The Rag

©2020 by Molly Britton

All rights reserved. No part of this may be reproduced, distributed or transmitted in any form or by any means without prior written permission.

These stories are works of fiction. Names, characters, places and incidents are the product of the author's imagination and are used fictitiously. Any resemblance to events, locales or actual persons, living or dead, is entirely coincidental.

Chapter 1

Chapter 2

Chapter 3

Chapter 4

Chapter 5

Chapter 6

Chapter 7

Chapter 8

Chapter 9

Chapter 10

Chapter 11

Chapter 12

More Victorian Romance

Chapter 1

Emma was lying in the sunshine of the small house, looking up at the sky. The clouds were passing through the sky quickly, and it looked like there might be a storm coming. She was happy, despite it, because her mother was due to come home early from work, and she had finished her chores early as well.

Emma sometimes watched the other children who walked past her small house and wondered what life would be like if she had been born into a different family. Other children went to school, rather than being stuck inside all day, doing chores. They walked down the street with their mothers and fathers, laughing in the sunshine.

Emma had no idea what it would be like to have both a mother and father walking down the street with her. Her father had died when she was born, and her mother had done the best she could to give Emma a life that she'd never had. Her mother worked overtime every day at the factory so that Emma would want for nothing, or so she said.

Emma wanted for lots of things, but she didn't tell her mother any of that. Instead, she told her mother that she was perfectly happy with everything she got and the life they had. And really, all she needed was a roof over her head, food in her stomach, and her mother there every day. Emma felt like she could get through anything if that was the case.

She heard a knock at the door and raised her head from where she was lying on the floor. They didn't have a chesterfield, only two wooden chairs, and so if she wanted to lie in the sunshine, it had to be on the floor.

She thought it was perhaps the milkman. He was an older man who sometimes came late in the day if he wasn't feeling well that day.

She stood up, and went to pull open the door, expecting to ask him if everything was all right.

To her surprise, it wasn't the milkman standing there at all. It was a man she had never met before, and he looked grim.

"Are you Emma Walker?" he asked.

"Y-yes," the twelve-year-old girl said, unsure of what was happening. Her mother had warned her about opening the door to strangers, especially given the fact that there had been a series of crimes in town, and Emma wondered if this was going to be one of those times.

"I need you to come with me," the man said, and Emma froze.

"Why?" she asked him.

"Because there's been an accident," he said. "You need to come down to the hospital."

Emma's mouth fell open.

"I can't … come to the hospital," she said, her mind not fully comprehending the situation. "I'm waiting for my mother to come home from work."

"Your mother is not coming home," the man said. "I work at the factory with her. She's had a very bad accident."

Emma didn't know what to do.

"My mother …" she said. "But … what happened?"

"One of the machines broke," the man said. "And she was under it."

Emma squeaked.

"Is she … Is she …"

"I work with her," he repeated, and his face was kind. "My name is Steven, and you need to come quickly if you wish to speak to your mother."

Emma was terrified. She didn't even know if she should take something from the house to the hospital. In her terrified child brain, she went into the kitchen and stuffed half a loaf of stale bread into her bag, just in case her mother was hungry. Then she followed Steven out of the house and onto the cobblestones.

"Your mother always talks about you at work," he said as they walked. "She speaks so fondly of you. She says that you're very smart and talented."

"At what?" Emma asked. She didn't think she was particularly good at anything.

Steven smiled.

"Well," he said. "She says that no matter what situation you're in, you can always find your way through it, even if it's an impassable mountain."

"Oh," Emma said quietly. "I suppose. That's kind of her. But why are you telling me this?"

"I just want you to be prepared," Steven said, and then they walked in silence until they reached the hospital.

***

Emma had never been to the hospital. She had heard stories about it, but she had never had reason to set foot into it. As soon as she got inside, she smelled horrible things. She had to hold her breath as Steven led her through a maze of hallways, and then, at long last, in to see her mother.

She almost didn't recognize her. She thought that she had been wearing a cream-coloured gown to go to work that morning, but now, it was deep red. It only took Emma half a second to discover that it was blood, and not the colour of the fabric. Her mother was lying on a bed and it seemed like she was barely breathing. She wasn't even looking at Emma, but her eyes were half open and she seemed to be mumbling.

"Mama?" she asked, reaching for her hand. She then realized that her hand was basically pulp. Emma began crying. "Mama!"

"Here," Steven said. "Look at her face. Look at her face and smile; she knows you're here. She knows that her daughter is going to be all right, doesn't she?"

"Please," Emma said, realizing the gravity of the situation. "Could I be alone with my mother, just for a little bit?"

"Of course," Steven said, and disappeared through the curtain. She then took a deep breath, and stepped forward, touching her mother's face.

"Mama?" she asked. "Mama, what am I supposed to do? Are you going to be all right? Mama, are you going to talk to me? Please? Please?"

Emma felt her mother take a deep breath, and she thought that maybe she was going to speak. But then a horrible feeling filled Emma and she screamed.

A few people came running. They pushed her aside, and Emma felt a change in the room, an odd presence, and then she felt it disappear. Her mother was gone; she knew that. She was truly alone in the world.

***

Emma didn't remember the next few hours. She knew that several doctors said that they were sorry, and that Steven offered to take her to her house. But then a kindly old woman showed up and suddenly Emma was sitting in the church sanctuary. She had no earthly idea how she got there, and she had no idea who had brought her there, because the old woman was no longer around.

"Emma," the priest said, coming to sit beside her. "Emma, dear, I'm so sorry to hear about your mother."

Father Jackson had known Emma since she was a little girl, and she trusted him. She always thought he was kind. However, that didn't take away the shock and pain she was feeling.

"I … I don't understand," Emma said. "She went to work this morning. She said that she would see me this afternoon … I finished my chores early because today was her half day … she can't be gone. How can she just be gone, Father?"

"God needed another angel," he said. "And so he called your mother home."

"No!" Emma howled, and threw herself into his arms. The tears were endless, and she couldn't stop them, no matter what she did. She knew that it was undignified, and her mother wouldn't approve, but Father Jackson didn't tell her to stop. Instead, he waited until she was a little more coherent, and then spoke softly.

"You are her only family," he said. "You have to help plan her funeral."

"What?" Emma said. "No, I can't do that. I can't—"

"You can," Father Jackson said to her. "You can and you will. You are strong."

"What will happen to me?" she asked.

"I'm not sure," Father Jackson said. "Do you have any money?"

Emma shook her head.

"And Mama was always talking about bills that need to be paid," she said.

"All right," he said. "I'm sure, my child, that there will be a solution. We just have to pray about it. Now, are you hungry? Tonight you can stay here in the church. There are a few others who are in a rough position who also stay here."

"No." She rubbed her eyes. "I want to be with my mother."

"My dear," the kindly priest said, "your mother is gone."

"I know," Emma said, trying to be brave. "But … if her funeral is going to be here, she's going to be brought here, isn't she?"

"Yes," he said. "Would that be a comfort for you?"

"It would," Emma said, trying to stop crying. "If these are truly my last few moments with her, I want to treasure them."

"I will arrange it," he said. "Is there anything else you need?"

"What …" Emma sniffled. "What should I do to plan her funeral?"

"I will bring you a book of hymns," the priest said. "And you can choose her favourites, as well as any flowers you want from the garden."

"All right," Emma nodded. "Mama would want me to … be prepared. Be organized. She always was."

"I will also look into your house," Father Jackson said. "To see if you are able to afford it with any money your mother left. I'm not sure if you will be allowed to stay, but we'll do our best."

"What if I can't stay?" she asked.

"Well … there is an orphanage," Father Jackson said.

She shook her head. "I don't know anything about the orphanage," she said.

"Except that mostly children younger than me go there."

"Children of all ages end up in the orphanage," Father Jackson said. "And they go on to live full lives. You'll be all right, Emma. Just have faith and pray as hard as you can. I have seen miracles from less."

Emma nodded. She had been praying this whole time, and it hadn't made any difference yet. However, she knew there was nothing else she could do. It was out of her hands.

Chapter 2

She didn't even own anything black. Emma had chosen her darkest blue dress for her mother's funeral, but it was ragged around the edges and she felt like her mother would be looking down disapprovingly. Emma felt like she hadn't slept in days, and she was cold and afraid as she sat in the first pew of the church during the funeral.

Her mother's colleagues attended the funeral, as did the neighbours. However, most of them sat farther back in the pews, and Emma felt alone as she sat on the front benches alone, normally reserved for family. She was all that was left of her parents' bloodline, and she had no idea what to do next. The priest had made it clear that while she could live in the church for a little while, she couldn't stay forever.

"We meet here today to honour the life of Gwendolyn Walker. We give thanks for her life and ask God to bless her now that her time in this world has come to an end."

The priest began the service and Emma noticed a woman walking in late. She didn't recognize her, keeping her head low and trying to hide the fact that she was crying. Her mother would have said it was undignified to cry in front of so many people, but Emma couldn't stop her own tears.

"For Gwendolyn Walker, the journey is now beginning. But for us, there is loss, grief, and pain. Every one of us here has been affected—perhaps in small ways, or perhaps in transformative ones—by Gwendolyn Walker. Her life mattered to us all."

To Emma's surprise, the woman that had walked in late came up to the front bench and sat down. Emma wasn't prepared for someone to sit so close to her, and scooted down. The woman smiled at her, and Emma took a moment to glance at her. She seemed well dressed, and she had a beautiful handbag in her lap. She didn't seem at all like the type of person who would attend her mother's funeral. They didn't know anyone so upper class.

"It is important for us to collectively acknowledge and accept that the world has fundamentally changed with her passing. We are all grieving. Life will not be the same—nor should it be. Together, let us open our hearts and commemorate the impact Gwendolyn Walker had on our lives."

"Hello, Emma," the woman said, and Emma reacted in surprise.

"How do you know my name?" she asked.

The woman raised an eyebrow with a smile. "Well, my dear," she said. "I've heard a lot about you, so I thought I should come and meet you myself."

At the front of the church, the priest commanded them to all bow their heads in prayer.

"Eternal God, we pray for ourselves and for Gwendolyn Walker. We stand where earth and heaven meet, where life is brought to death. Deliver us from grief, fear, and doubt, from despair and unbelief, and bring us to the light of your presence. Grant us that peace which the world cannot give so that we, with Gwendolyn Walker, may trust in you and find our life through you. Lord, you renew the face of the earth. Gather to yourself Gwendolyn Walker, whom we have loved, and grant her those things which eye has not seen, nor ear heard, nor the human heart imagined. Great God, watch over us this day and all days."

"Such a sad day," the woman said to her. "For there is no one to watch over you now, is there?"

Emma felt her heart all over again break at those words. She knew it to be true, of course, but she hadn't yet allowed herself to say them out loud.

"No," she said quietly. "There isn't anyone. But Father Jackson said I could stay here for a time—"

"Tut tut, dear," the woman said. "A church rectory is no place for a child. You should be with other children. Wouldn't you like that?"

Emma looked at her curiously.

"I've never ... been somewhere with other children," she said. "It was always just Mama and me."

"What a shame," the woman said. "I have a place where there are other children around all the time. Wouldn't you like that?"

"Give us the strength to accept what is past, to appreciate what is present, and to look forward to good in our future. Grant us peace, sacred moments of communion with the universe, and faith in whatever most expresses our deepest inner truth. Bless us and heal us; breathe peace and grace into our lives. Amen. Please stand."

Emma scrambled to her feet, but couldn't stop looking over at the woman as Father Jackson led them all in prayer.

"Gwendolyn Walker is now safe. She is already on her way to heaven to enjoy all which awaits there. Let us say this final farewell to her body as we commit Gwendolyn Walker's physical form to its natural end."

"How did you know that I was here?" she asked the woman, who smiled.

"Well, I run the orphanage," she said, and Emma bristled at the word. "And I try to keep an eye out for all poor lost souls like you. You are in a very unfortunate situation, my dear, but that doesn't mean that it can't be turned around. Everything is going to be all right."

"Gwendolyn Walker, we bless you and thank you for being a part of our lives. We honour your life on Earth and we pray for your peace ever-after. We will not forget you. Go well into the kingdom of heaven. Please sit."

Emma sat down, considering her options. The woman did seem very kind and she was very well dressed. And she was right; Emma could not stay in the church forever. However, she was leery of the fact that it was an orphanage, and she hadn't heard wonderful stories about such a place.

"We have been remembering with love and gratitude a life that touched us all. I encourage you to help, support, and love those who grieve most. Allow them to cry, to hurt, to smile, and to remember. Grief works through our systems in its own time. Remember to bless each day and to live it to the fullest in honour of life itself and of Gwendolyn Walker. We often take life for granted and yet it is the greatest gift God gave us."

***

Emma was so lost in her own thoughts that she barely noticed when the funeral ended. People came up to hug her and offer their blessings and yet the woman stayed steadily beside her.

"What is your name?" Emma asked at last.

"Mrs. Joffrey," she said. "And I think we are going to get to know each other quite well."

Emma saw Father Jackson coming towards her with a smile on his face.

"Ah, Emma," he said. "I see that you've met Mrs. Joffrey."

"You know her?" Emma asked. Her opinion of the woman improved by the fact that Father Jackson seemed to offer his recommendation.

"Yes," he said. "I contacted her just after your mother died. I told you that we'd find a place for you."

"It's quite a nice place too," Mrs. Joffrey said. "With so many other children. Would you like that? I can promise you a warm place to stay, as well as three meals a day. What do you think?"

"I …" Emma said, looking between the woman and Father Jackson. Even though she was a bit nervous, it wasn't as if she had anything else to do. "All right."

"Wonderful." Mrs. Joffrey's face lit up.

"But … can we go to the graveyard first?" Emma asked, and Mrs. Joffrey shook her head as if she had forgotten.

"Of course," she said. "And then pack your things."

Emma didn't have many things to pack, given that her mother's house had been rented and they'd barely had enough money to feed themselves.

***

The dirt on her mother's grave was barely settled before Mrs. Joffrey indicated she should get ready to leave. Emma gathered up her small bag and then said goodbye to Father Jackson. Mrs. Joffrey had a carriage waiting, and Emma slipped in quietly.

The carriage door shut and Mrs. Joffrey sat opposite her. Emma found the courage to ask her a question as the carriage rolled along.

"How long have you been running an orphanage?" she asked.

"A long time," Mrs. Joffrey said, and Emma felt the carriage suddenly grow cold.

"Thank you for offering me this chance," Emma said. "I didn't know what I would do without any money."

"Oh, you'll earn your keep," Mrs. Joffrey said. "Don't think you won't."

"Oh," Emma said. "Of course. I always did chores for Mama, so I'm sure that will be all right."

"Yes," Mrs. Joffrey said. "If you claim to have experience, then you won't fail at the tasks I give you."

"What kind of tasks?" Emma asked.

"You'll see," Mrs. Joffrey said, and didn't say anything the rest of the ride.

Emma felt sudden fear in the pit of her stomach and wondered if she had done something to anger the woman. She had seemed so friendly not so long ago, and Emma clutched her bag against her chest, a bit worried.

When they got to the orphanage, Emma thought it was beautiful. It was a big house, and she imagined that she would feel a sense of peace once she got inside. However, that dream was shattered the second that Emma walked in.

The inside of the house was nowhere near as grand as the outside. There was a strange energy in the house, and there were several ratty-looking children inside. When they looked up to Emma, they didn't look excited. They just looked sad.

"Maybell!" Mrs. Joffrey snapped, and a girl no older than Emma came forward.

"Show Emma a bed. And then bring her back down here immediately."

"Yes, ma'am," Maybell said, and got up from where she was scrubbing the floor. Emma, although shy, wasn't necessarily afraid of making new friends, and she tried to smile at the girl.

"Hello," she said as the girl showed her upstairs. "My name is Emma."

"Why would you come here, Emma?" the girl asked her, and Emma's eyes widened.

"I … my mother just died," she said. "I had nowhere else to go."

"This is worse than having nowhere else to go," she said. "Worse than everything."

"What?" Emma asked. "What do you mean? Mrs. Joffrey seems so nice."

Maybell burst out laughing, and shook her head.

"She's not nice," she said. "She's a monster. She hates us."

"Surely that can't be true," Emma said as Maybell led her into a room with about twenty beds. The sheets looked thin and threadbare and the pillows were barely fluffed. They were practically flat against the thin mattress. "She came to get me from my mother's funeral."

"She wants more children to work for her," Maybell said. "And if you do anything wrong, you will pay for it."

"I … don't have any money," Emma said, and Maybell shook her head.

"She doesn't want money. Although if you make any money, she will take it. But if you don't have any and you've done something wrong, she will beat you or make you do chores all night long."

Emma froze. "Is that … No, you're jesting, aren't you?"

Maybell's face, however, told Emma that she wasn't joking.

"I thought she was kind too," she said. "She came to my father's funeral."

"Oh." Emma felt like crying.

"You can use this bed." Maybell pointed to the bed in the corner. "It used to be Sarah's."

"What happened to Sarah?" Emma asked, afraid to hear the answer.

"She was sent away," Maybell said. "Lucky her."

"Oh," Emma said.

"Come downstairs in five minutes," Maybell said, and left her alone in the room. Emma sat down on the bed, trying to make sense of what had just happened. Had she been tricked? Was this all a nightmare?

She had barely unpacked her things when she heard a child scream in pain downstairs. Mrs. Joffrey was yelling something and then Emma heard something hit the floor. She closed her eyes, tears streaking down her face. This was not the way her life was supposed to be.

She unpacked the rest of her things quickly, and then hurried down the stairs. There was a young boy sitting in the corner with a bloody nose, staring at the wall. The other children, who were scrubbing the floor, deliberately ignored him.

"Emma," Mrs. Joffrey said, turning to her with a smile that now sent a chill down Emma's spine. "Are you hungry?"

"Yes, ma'am," Emma said.

"Well, supper is in six hours," Mrs. Joffrey said. "And if you'd like some, I'd like those stairs to sparkle."

"The … stairs?" Emma turned back and looked at the giant staircase she had just come down. The stairs weren't exactly filthy, but cleaning them seemed like an impossible task. Emma was exhausted, and she felt like she could cry a river.

"Do you not understand English?" Mrs. Joffrey asked. "Father Jackson didn't tell me you were slow."

"I'm ... what would you like me to clean the stairs with?" Emma asked.

"What would you like me to clean the stairs with?" Mrs. Joffrey mocked her. "A bucket of water and a rag, child. What do you think?"

"I'll show you," Maybell got up from the floor, indicating that Emma should follow her. Emma knew better than to argue. She followed Maybell to the kitchen, where there were several buckets already filled. Maybell silently pointed to a pile of rags, and added some soap to a bucket for her. Emma picked up a rag and then the bucket, following Maybell back to the stairs.

"Thank you," Emma whispered to her silently, and Maybell nodded. Emma put the rag in the bucket, and started on the first stair.

"I want them to sparkle," Mrs. Joffrey said to her. "Do you understand?"

"Yes, ma'am," Emma said, trying not to cry. She glanced at the boy in the corner, who was still wiping blood from his nose. She didn't think that there was anything worse than her mother dying. However, this was what she imagined the Bible warned about. This was her version of hell, and she knew that she had to get out of this situation as soon as possible. She didn't know when, and she didn't know how, but she couldn't stay. She wouldn't survive.

Chapter 3

Emma saw her opportunity a few weeks later. Mrs. Joffrey was usually always in the orphanage, spending her days ordering people around and beating those who disobeyed. Despite the fact that Emma had been promised three meals a day, she only got one—if she was lucky. She was already thin, and she didn't have any weight to lose, but she lost several pounds in the few weeks that she lived in the orphanage. She was starving, she was exhausted, and she had been beaten twice by Mrs. Joffrey for not doing a perfect job with her chores. Her wrists throbbed and her head was in a constant fog.

But today there was a reprieve of sorts. Mrs. Joffrey was on the hunt for an older male child to do some of the heavier chores, and she had gotten word of one in the west end of the city. She instructed the children to clean the entire house and threatened their very lives if they didn't. And then, to Emma's delight, she walked out the door.

As soon as she did, Emma went upstairs to pack her things.

"What are you doing?" Maybell asked in horror.

"I'm leaving," Emma said. "And if you know what is good for you, you'll leave too. This is no way to live."

"But …" Maybell looked at her in horror. "We can't just leave. Mrs. Joffrey will beat us."

"Not if she can't find us," Emma said. "Will you come with me?"

Maybell took a moment, and then shook her head.

"No," she said. "I can't."

"Why not?" Emma asked.

"I can't," Maybell said. "I have nowhere else to go."

"Neither do I," Emma said. "But anywhere is better than here."

"I can't," she said again, and Emma sighed as she picked up her bag.

"Well … thank you for everything you've done to help me," she said. "I will miss you."

"Good luck to you," Maybell said, and the two girls hugged.

Emma said goodbye to a few more children, and then she slipped out the door, looking both ways on the street to make sure that she didn't see Mrs. Joffrey coming back. Her heart was beating at what felt like a thousand beats a minute, and she crossed the street quickly, getting farther away from the orphanage with each step.

***

It was only an hour before Emma realized that while she had taken a bag of clothes and a few trinkets, she didn't have any money or any food. She didn't even know where she could get a drink to wet her parched mouth. She was very happy that she wasn't going to be beaten by Mrs. Joffrey anymore, but she didn't know how she was going to survive on the cold street.

Emma walked up and down the main street, cursing herself for not thinking through her plan a little more clearly. Eventually, she sat down on a bench, trying to think through her next move. She was cold and tired, and she would give anything for a small glass of water.

She saw a few other children on the street, and at first, she thought they were just playing, or were lost, or orphans like her. However, the more she watched, the more she realized that they were working.

The children seemed to know each other, but they were trying to avoid talking to each other. They were walking up and down the main street, pretending to be distracted as they walked. However, they were walking down the street very close to certain people, who, Emma noted, were dressed very well. After walking behind them for a while, the children would peel off, go to an older child, and hand him something. Then they would go back and find another person to follow.

It took Emma a little while to realize that they were pickpockets. They were going into handbags and pockets and taking coin purses, money, and valuables. And from what she could see, they were very successful.

Emma didn't know what to do. She could report them to the police, but she didn't know that the police would believe her. She was just as ragged and young as they were, and she didn't want to get in any trouble, given that she already had no idea what she was going to do and where she was going to go.

Just as she decided to get away from the thieves and not be associated with them, just in case the police came along, she saw the older child go into a bakery. Five minutes later, he came out with bags and bags of food. All the children swarmed around him, and he handed out food until it looked like they each had a feast. Emma watched in shock with her stomach growling as they all sat down on the street corner and began to eat. Her mouth watered and her eyes widened, imagining the taste of the pastries in her mouth.

She felt faint with hunger, watching them eat, and she decided to leave the area in case she lost control and pounced on them. She hadn't eaten since the day before, and she wasn't sure how much longer she could go on.

Just as she got up, one of them noticed her.

"Hey," the older child called. "Come on over if you're hungry."

Emma froze.

"Me?" she asked.

"Yes, you," he said. "Come on over; we have more than enough to share."

Despite the fact that she knew the food had been acquired by questionable means, she found herself unable to control her legs. She was propelled towards them, her mouth watering.

"My name is Talan," the boy said. "What's your name?"

"Emma," she said, hovering at the edge of the impromptu circle.

"Well, Emma, you look hungry," he said. "Would you like to sit down?"

Emma swallowed hard.

"I saw what you did," she said. "I saw how you got it."

"We bought it," Talan said and Emma felt her palms get sweaty.

"Yes, but you … took money from …"

"We took money from people who have more than enough," Talan said. "And they won't miss it. They have so many things that I promise they won't even notice."

"But you stole," Emma said. "That's wrong."

"Is it?" Talan asked. "Because we would starve to death without that money. And the Bible does say to share with the poor. And you're poor, aren't you, Emma?"

She nodded mutely.

"Do you not have parents?" one of the children asked.

"No," Emma said, her lip trembling. "I never knew my father and my mother … died."

"That is the situation with most of us," Talan said. "Do you have a home?"

"I just … I was in an orphanage," she said. "But I ran away."

"Sit down," Talan said, offering her a pastry. "There's nothing wrong with having just one."

Emma couldn't resist. She sat down and ripped into the pastry, devouring it in a very undignified fashion. She knew that her mother would be embarrassed if she saw her, but Emma couldn't control herself. Once she finished the first one, Talan handed her another. Emma finally started to feel like she wasn't going to swoon as she sat there. Eventually, she felt her mood lift and her mind started to clear.

"How long ago did your mother die?" Talan asked.

"A few weeks ago," Emma said. "Mrs. Joffrey at the orphanage came to get me, and I thought that I would be safe there, but …"

"Orphanages are never a safe place," Talan said. "That's why many of us are here. We are looking out for each other."

"How …" Emma thought about her question carefully. "How do you not get caught?"

"Practice," Talan said. "And the fact that most people just yell at us and walk off. They won't call the police. Especially if you're a girl."

"What?" Emma asked.

"It's true," a young girl spoke up. "I'm so good at it because most people don't expect it."

"How long have you been doing this?" Emma asked, and Talan shrugged.

"For some of us, it's been a few years," he said. "It's really not that hard."

"But where do you sleep?" she asked.

"Mostly out here," he said, and she gasped. He laughed. "It's really not as bad as it seems. We've carved out some good places to protect us from the elements. And it's much more comfortable than any hard, half-broken orphanage bed."

She couldn't believe she was having this conversation.

"Look," Talan said. "Why don't you just stay with me and watch for a bit? If you want to join us, I'm sure we can make room for one more. And if you don't want to join us, you can be on your way."

Emma was wary of their kindness about Mrs. Joffrey's display.

"Why would you take me in?" she asked. "Why are you being so kind to me? You don't know me."

"That is true," Talan said. "But all of us were like you once. And we have to look out for each other, because there is no one to look out for us."

Emma considered this.

"My mother died when I was ten," Talan said. "And I never knew my father either."

"I'm sorry," Emma said. "How did she die?"

"Accident at a factory she worked at," Talan said and Emma's eyes widened.

"That's how my mother died too," she said, and Talan nodded.

"The factories are very dangerous and no one looks out for each other there. That's part of the reason we try extra hard to look out for each other here."

Emma remained silent, trying to weigh her options. She was worried that the children would take advantage of her like Mrs. Joffrey had. However, she really did not have another option. Her few hours on the street had proven that she had no idea how to take care of herself out here.

"Just watch," Talan said. "You don't have to decide right now."

Since all the food was eaten, the rest of the children got up and separated from their large group, heading back out in the street.

Emma stayed with Talan and watched them work. It only took her a little while to see that it was truly an art form that took skill. They were careful about who they choose to follow, and they sometimes worked in teams, one distracting and one pickpocketing. She was in awe of the trust that they had in Talan, handing over every penny and trinket to his waiting hands.

"Because we have to take care of each other," Talan said to her. "And I'm not very good at pickpocketing, to tell you the truth. We're a team."

"Are you successful … every day?" Emma asked.

"Haven't been hungry in all the years I've been out here," Talan said. "And most nights, I'm warm and comfortable. It's not exactly easy, but I wouldn't say it's the worst thing in the world. There are many people in worse positions than us."

***

As the sun set, the children began to return to Talan, one by one. He turned to Emma with a smile as the last one joined their group.

"What do you think?" he said. Emma's stomach was growling again for dinner, and it was starting to grow cold outside. "Will you join us?"

"Perhaps for a little while," Emma said at last.

"Great!" Talan said. "Why don't we get some supper, and then we'll show you where we're sleeping tonight?"

"All right," Emma agreed as Talan counted the money that they had gotten.

"Where should we go for supper?" he asked the children, who had many suggestions. Emma couldn't believe their suggestions; places she had never thought to dine at. She didn't think she would ever be able to afford such a place, even when her mother was alive. Perhaps this life was going to work out after all. In any case, it wasn't as if she had anywhere else to go.

Chapter 4

Emma should have known better. She told herself that every night she slept in a cold warehouse, or under a bridge. She told herself that she was stupid for trusting; she was stupid for believing an unbelievable situation. She was just stupid, heartbroken, and trapped.

Talan had not portrayed the situation as accurate. He had said that they shared everything, and that they were well fed and well looked after. However, that wasn't exactly true. There was a level above Talan in terms of the organization, and they were not kind. They took a percentage of the money, which Talan secretly kept to hand over. And if the children didn't steal enough, they were beaten, yelled at, and made to sleep in the worst spot. In a lot of ways, the streets were where they had the most freedom. If they stole enough, everything was rosy. But if they didn't, it was miserable. Emma didn't see that side the first day, but soon it became obvious that her life here was not going to be much better than the orphanage. After three years, she felt like her soul was dying.

She would never trust anyone again; she was certain of that. She would keep her heart and her mind protected, and do whatever she needed to do to survive. Trust was not an option for people like her, and she accepted that now. She saw couples holding hands on the street and wondered how they trusted the other to not take their wallet or randomly hit them and run off with everything they held dear. She only had her bag of belongings for a few days before it was stolen and sold, with a hefty percentage going towards the oldest of the children, who ran the den of thieves like a shady business.

Emma cried herself to sleep most nights and did everything she could to wipe her mind of anything during the day. She felt like she was walking underwater, and like she was living a half-life. It was terrible, and she wasn't sure living was better than dying.

On a rainy Tuesday, after a night of no sleep, when her head felt foggy, she made an almost fatal mistake. She wasn't paying attention and wasn't as sneaky as she normally was. She was about to pick the pocket of a wealthy man when he suddenly spun around.

"What the hell are you doing, you little thief?" the man said. He was dressed very well, and Emma was certain that he wouldn't even miss what she was about to take.

"I … nothing?" she said. Technically, she hadn't even taken anything.

"I know what you are doing," he said. "Trying to pick my pocket. I could have you thrown in jail. "

"No …" Emma said. "I haven't done anything."

"I don't think the police will care that you are rubbish at pickpocketing," he said. "They will arrest you and throw you in the stocks."

Emma's lip started to tremble. She knew what was going to happen if she didn't come back with a certain amount of money by lunchtime.

"I …"

"Sir." Suddenly, there was another man standing in the street. He was much younger than the man Emma had tried to rob, but just as well dressed. Emma guessed that he was only a few years older. "No harm done, don't you agree?"

The older gentleman stared at the younger one.

"Who are you?" he asked.

"My name is Lucas," he said. "I don't know you and you don't know me. But if you look at this young girl, you can see that she is sad and starving. She is thin and ragged and probably has no one. Surely we can be a bit more generous with our time and money, can't we?"

"Absolutely not," the man said. "How do I know she has not taken off with something else of mine just because my coin purse is still here? I'm going to fetch the police."

"Now hold on," Lucas said. "Why don't I give you a little something to forget everything?"

The man sputtered, and Emma thought he was going to refuse. But instead, he smiled.

"Oh really?" he said. "How do I know that you're not in league with her?"

"I've never met him before," Emma protested, in awe of this young man's kindness. "Never. But sir, you really don't have to do this. I …"

"Don't be silly," the man said. "This is my choice. Now, how much will it take?"

Emma watched the two of them have a brief conversation, and then Lucas handed over a wad of notes. The older man counted them, and then smirked.

"Fine with me," he said, and took off down the street.

Emma turned to Lucas in shock. If she hadn't been so scared, she might have noticed that he was quite handsome. He had dark hair and green eyes, and he was dressed in a well-tailored suit that showed off his lean, muscular figure. She guessed that he was around twenty years old, and he had a beautiful smile.

"Why did you do that?" she asked him.

He shrugged. "Well," he said. "My mother always taught me to be kind. And I thought that you had an honest face. You wouldn't be doing this unless you needed to, isn't that true?"

"I …" Emma felt ashamed. "Yes."

"Well," he said, looking her up and down. "I was actually on my way to place an advertisement in the paper. For a housemaid."

"Oh," Emma said, not sure what this had to do with her.

"But," he said. "Perhaps you'd like to save me the trip?"

"You want me to place the advertisement for you?" Emma asked, confused.

"No," Lucas said. "I was wondering if you'd like to come work with me at my house."

"What?" Emma answered, stunned. She had no idea why he would ask such a thing. "Me?"

"Sure," Lucas said. "I have other housemaids, and they could easily teach you the job."

"Why would you ask me that?" she said. "You've seen how I make my living. How do you know I won't rob you blind?"

"I don't," he said with a kind smile. "But I have a feeling that tough exterior is only to protect yourself. You can trust me."

Emma bristled at that word.

"No," she said. "I can't."

The man's smile didn't falter, and he reached in his pocket, pulling out a calling card.

"Very well," he said. "But at least take my calling card, in case you need to contact me. In case you change your mind."

"I won't change my mind," Emma said, but took the card anyways. It was edged in what looked like gold and she briefly wondered if she could sell it for a coin.

"That's up to you," he said. "It was lovely to meet you …"

"Emma," she said, wondering why she said that. She didn't tell anyone her name anymore. The few souls who wanted to save her reminded her of Mrs. Joffrey's false smile, and she didn't want anyone to remind her of her life before that. Even her name was tainted with memories of her mother.

"Well, Emma," he said. "I hope to see you again."

With that, he walked off. Emma watched him go, unsure of what to feel. An old part of her wanted to trust him, but she had promised herself that she would never trust again. She bit her lip and turned around, looking for another victim. However, her mind was distracted, and she was not very successful at all. When she returned to the meeting point, she knew she was going to be in trouble.

"Very good, everyone," Talan was saying as he took their earnings. "Very good. And Emma?"

"I ... couldn't do anything today," she said, fearful of what was to come. She looked down the street, and to her horror, saw the heads of their organization walking towards them. Sometimes they met up like this, to make sure Talan wasn't stealing from them as well. "I got caught and then …"

"You got caught?" Talan asked, raising his eyebrows. "That's not like you."

"I know, it's just …"

"I don't think you got caught," he said as the oldest ones approached. "Emma is withholding money."

"Talan!" she said in shock. "I'm not …"

"Oh, Emma is withholding money?" Michael, the head of the thieves, said. "Well, we know what happens to people who withhold money."

"Please." Emma felt tears pouring down her face. She was so frustrated with the fact that she was crying. She had been so emotionally guarded these last few years, and she had hardly cried in front of other people. "Please …"

"Everyone watch," Michael said as he took a step closer to Emma. "And we'll show you what happens when people withhold money."

Emma felt a slap across the face and she knew there was no getting away. She braced herself for a kick and then another one. Normally, it was just a few kicks or a slap and it was done. But Michael seemed to be in a terrible mood, and he hit her again and again and again. Emma fell to the ground, seeing stars. She felt like she couldn't breathe, and there was blood pouring out of her nose.

"Please," she whimpered. "Please, stop. I haven't … please stop."

Her cries got weaker and weaker. No one helped her, or even spoke up. Emma felt a blow to her head, and she closed her eyes. Another blow to the head knocked her unconscious, and she was almost grateful for it.

***

When Emma awoke, she had no idea how long she had been out. She didn't recognize where she was at first. She only knew that she hurt everywhere, and she was very cold.

It took a while before her vision stabilized, and she saw that she was in the same back alley that she had met everyone in. She was lying on the ground, and her face felt sticky. There was blood on her hands, and she couldn't open one eye properly. It was dark, and she only knew she wasn't dead because she hurt so much.

Emma lay on the ground for quite a while before she slowly managed to sit up. Nothing was broken, but she felt incredibly ill. She was alone, and the moon was high in the sky. She must have been lying there for hours.

There was no way she could go back to the group now. They had beaten someone once like this before, and Emma had never seen them again.

She couldn't even consider going to the orphanage. She wasn't sure that Mrs. Joffrey would take her back, and even if she did, that life wasn't much better.

Emma was truly alone, and hopeless.

Her nose was running, and she reached into her pocket, hoping for a handkerchief. There wasn't a handkerchief, but there was something odd in her pocket. Pulling it out, she saw that it was a calling card from Lucas, the man that had been so kind to her. It was crumpled and smeared with blood, and her vision was blurry, but she could just make out the address on it.

She didn't know what to do. She was freezing, she was exhausted, and she wasn't sure she could even walk. But there was nowhere else to go and she knew that she couldn't survive on her own. Her only skill was pickpocketing, and if they saw her working on her own, they would beat her again, or worse.

She was out of options. She had to trust again, even if it ended up killing her.

Chapter 5

Emma didn't know how she managed to get up and make it to Lucas's town house, but she somehow did. The town house was quite a nice one, and she felt embarrassed to be knocking on the door. Her limbs were trembling and she wasn't sure she could stand up much longer. She pounded on the door several times, praying that someone would open the door soon. Already, some people on the street had given her odd looks, and she feared for her safety. She imagined she looked quite disgusting, and she wondered whether people thought she was a lady of the night, all roughed up. She needed to be inside more than she worried about whether or not Lucas could be trusted.

Finally, the door opened, and there was a sleepy-looking woman standing on the other side.

"Can I help you?"

"My—my name is Emma," she said. "I met Mr. Lucas earlier today. He said to come by if I ever needed any help."

The woman raised her eyebrows.

"Is that so?" she said. "Did he say to come by before dawn?"

"No," Emma said, her lip trembling. "But I ... please, I need help."

The woman started to close the door.

"I don't think so," she said, and the tears flowed over Emma's face.

"He did," she said. "He really, really did, please, he said that if I ..."

"Shauna, what is happening?" She heard Lucas' voice on the stairs behind the woman. The woman pulled open the door again, looking guilty.

"Nothing, sir," she said. "This young woman is trying to ..."

"Emma," he said. He was wearing a dressing robe and looked half asleep, but he clearly recognized her. "What happened to you? Is everything all right?"

"Yes," Emma sniffled. "No. I don't know what to do."

"You know her?" Shauna asked, and Lucas nodded.

"Yes," he said. "I offered her assistance today. Please, Emma, come in."

He was holding a candle and when Emma stepped into its light, he gasped.

"Oh my Lord," he said.

"I just … I didn't make enough money today," she said. "They didn't believe me, they thought I was hoarding it and …"

"Yes," Lucas said. "I think I understand. I'm so sorry. Had I known that was the case when I …"

"No, it's not your fault," Emma said, wiping her nose. "It's not …"

"You must stay here tonight," Lucas said. "We will get you some fresh clothes and get you cleaned up. Everything is going to be all right."

"Really?" Emma said. She didn't want to trust Lucas, but she was so tired and so cold. She didn't have any fight left in her. If Lucas wasn't who he said he was, she wouldn't be able to run again. As far as she was concerned, this was the end of the road for her.

She wasn't sure whether she could even make it up the stairs. But she somehow followed the woman named Shauna, who was Lucas' head housemaid. The woman didn't say much, but she did offer her a cool cloth and fresh clothes.

"Don't worry," Shauna said at last, when Emma finally felt a little more human. "He does this a lot."

"He does what a lot?" Emma asked, confused and exhausted.

"The master takes in pity cases all the time," Shauna said. "And he turns them around."

Emma knew that maybe she should take offense to that comment, but she didn't.

"What do you mean, turns them around?"

"He's taken in quite a few boys over the years from the streets," Shauna said. "They worked as stable boys and as footmen, and some of them are quite respectable now. One of them even works in a law office."

"Ah," Emma said. "So … I'm just a pity case."

"There's nothing wrong with taking a leg up," Shauna said to her. "You can sleep here."

She showed Emma to a small room and Emma's eyes widened. There was a bed that looked warm and fluffy and a beautiful quilt on top of it.

"All by myself?" Emma said, and Shauna raised her eyebrows.

"Did you want someone to stay with you?" she asked.

"No," Emma blushed. "It's just I've never … never had a room to myself."

"Never?" Shauna said.

"Well, when I lived with my mother," she said. "But that was many years ago."

"What happened to your mother?" Shauna asked, with some pity.

"She died," Emma said. "A very long time ago."

"I'm sorry," Shauna said. "That is the case with so many."

Emma didn't say anything, her body aching for a bed. Shauna eventually left her alone, and Emma lay down, closing her eyes. For the moment, everything seemed perfect.

***

When she opened her eyes again, it was suddenly morning. Emma had no idea how long she slept, but the birds were chirping and the sun was shining. No one had knocked on her door, but she could smell food cooking downstairs.

When she sat up, she wasn't in as much pain as the night before. She was still very sore, but she managed to wash at the basin that had been left for her on the nightstand, and changed into a rough cotton shift and dress that had also been left for her. Somehow, it fit, despite the fact that she had never seen it before. She couldn't believe that someone would be so kind. She was sure that there was a catch.

She came down the stairs carefully, worried about falling. When she got into the dining room, she found Lucas sitting there, enjoying a breakfast full of eggs and sausage.

"Hello, Emma," Lucas said with a smile. "How did you sleep?"

"I slept all right," Emma replied. "I'll be out of your—"

"What?" Lucas asked in surprise. "Where are you going?"

"You … you don't want me to go?" she asked.

"You are in no condition to go," he said. "You need to stay until you are fully healed."

"I have no money," Emma said. "And I don't think I could work yet …"

"It's all right," Lucas said. "I am fully prepared to offer you room and board until you are fully healed. After that, you can decide what you would like to do. If you want to stay, that's all right. And if you want to go, you don't have to feel obligated to work here."

"Why would you do this?" Emma asked, and Lucas smiled.

"Miss Emma, I don't think badly of you because of the circumstances we met in," he said. "I believe that those who go into a life of crime do it for two reasons. Either they have a dark soul or they are there out of necessity. I believe that you were committing such crimes simply because you had no other option."

Emma hung her head. She didn't know what to say to that.

"And looking at you now, this morning," he said, "I believe that even more."

Emma looked up at him then.

"What do you want from me?" she asked.

"I know that many people have probably hurt you before," he said. "But I promise that I do not want anything of you. I simply want you to recover and to have a second chance at the life you want."

"Thank you," Emma said, although she wasn't entirely sure that she trusted him.

"Good," Lucas said. "Now that that is settled, may I offer you some breakfast?"

"Yes, please," she said, staring at the food in front of them. Her mouth was practically watering, and Lucas got up to pull out a chair for her.

"I have asked the doctor to step in and have a look at you later today," he said. "I hope you don't mind."

"I would appreciate that," Emma said as she saw the extent of the bruising on her hands in the sunlight. "Is this … your house?"

"Indeed it is," he said. She was practically shoving food in her mouth, but he didn't say a word.

"How can you … afford this?" she asked, swallowing. "Apologies if that is rude. I mean … do you have money? Family money?"

"My father has done well for himself as a merchant," he said. "But I work as barrister."

"Oh my," she said. She had never met someone in such a respectable position. "That sounds quite exciting."

"It can be, some days," he said with a shrug. "Other days it's simply a lot of paperwork."

"Am I keeping you from work today?" she said. "Please do not stay here on my account."

"I'm not staying on your account," he assured her. "Today is my day off."

"Oh my," she blushed. "And I woke you up in the middle of the night when you need rest after a long work week."

"It's nothing," he assured her. "Really. I don't sleep much. My mind is always active."

"What do you think about?" she asked, and then realized that was too personal for a man she had just met. "My apologies."

He smiled.

"Not at all," he said. "I mostly think about the cases I have at work, or the people I am trying to help, both at work and … not on the job."

"Yes, Miss Shauna said that you offer your assistance often," she said. "God bless you."

"I hope one day he does," Lucas said with a shrug. "But that is not why I do it. I simply believe that we were put on this earth to help each other, and this is what I can do."

He and Emma finished breakfast together, and she soon felt exhausted from the effort of coming down stairs. He urged her to head back and rest, and told her the doctor would be along shortly.

***

Emma was grateful to crawl back into her warm bed, not even bothering to undress. The doctor did come around shortly, and he told her that while she was bruised, nothing was broken, and she would make a full recovery. He encouraged her to rest, take in sunshine, and eat well.

"Have you …" Emma asked shyly. "Do you have to come to this house often?"

"Yes," the doctor said. "I often come to see some of the folks that Mr. Lucas takes in. He seems to have a knack for finding the ones that need the most help. And from the looks of you, miss, you wouldn't have lasted too much longer on the streets."

``I made a mistake," Emma said, feeling the tears coming again.

"Perhaps you did," said the doctor. "But you started to repair it by accepting help. You'll be all right."

"Thank you," she said, lying back down. There was a knock on the door and Shauna entered, carrying a tray.

"Mr. Lucas said you had taken to your bed, so I brought you a tray for lunch," Shauna said. "Please eat whatever you like."

"I am sorry for waking you up in the middle of the night," Emma said.

The housemaid shrugged. "It's all right," she said. "We just have to be careful about the people we let in. There are some dangerous folks out on the streets."

"Yes, I know," Emma said softly.

"Of course you do," Shauna said. "Now, if you need anything at all, just shout."

"Thank you," Emma said. "No one has been kind to me in so long."

"You will be expected to work eventually," Shauna said. "But when you are ready."

"I know," Emma said. "I used to do chores for my mother and …" The tears came in a fresh flood and she put her hands up to her face to stop them.

Shauna put the tray on the nightstand and went to close the door.

"It's all right," she said. "For now, just rest."

She left Emma alone in the room, and eventually, the tears stopped. Maybe, Emma thought, just maybe, this was where she belonged. Maybe at last, this was someone she could trust. In any case, she had a warm bed and food in her stomach, and that was more than she had had in a long time. She was going to enjoy it while it lasted. Eventually, as she had learned in life, everything was bound to turn sour.

Chapter 6

It was several weeks before Emma felt like herself again. Slowly, the bruises started to recede and she began to have an easier time walking. She spent less time crying and more time laughing. She gained some weight and her face gained some colour. She started to speak more, showing her personality, and she stopped looking over her shoulder at every opportunity. She smiled whenever someone came into the room, and she felt at ease in the home that she was in. The best part of all was that Lucas seemed to not be anything except the person he said he was. He was a kindhearted soul who truly wanted to help people, and Emma couldn't believe her luck.

One afternoon, when he came in the door early from work, Emma was sitting in the garden reading.

"I was wondering," he said to her, startling her. "My apologies."

"No, it's my fault," Emma said. "I am still a bit …"

"It's all right," he said. "I was just going to see if you wanted to accompany me on a stroll into town."

"M-me?" she said, in shock.

"Yes," he said. "The doctor said that it would be good for you to start walking some distance, and while you have recovered while here, you must start to regain your strength with more than reading."

"Of course," she said. "I understand if you want me to start working …"

"Emma," he held up his hand. "I don't wish for such a thing. I just need to go into town and I thought you'd enjoy coming."

"I …" she swallowed hard. "There are people in town … that …"

"I will keep you safe," he promised her, offering his arm. "I promise."

She wavered for a moment, and then stood up.

"I would very much like that," she said, putting her book down on the chair. She was grateful that her mother had taught her to read, because such stories were often her only escape. She wasn't a very strong reader and it took her a long time to get through a book of fables, but she savoured every moment. "Thank you."

She took his arm as they went out the back gate, and the path that led to the centre of town.

"I've never asked how long you've lived here?" she asked him. "The house seems very much to your tastes."

"Two years," he said. "It was my first purchase, as soon as I was able."

"Your parents must be so proud of you," she said, and he shrugged.

"I think it was what was expected," he said, slowing his pace when he realized he was causing her breath to come in slight gasps. She was almost at full strength, but she hadn't been walking since she was a pickpocket, and her face was losing colour. He kept an eye on her as they strolled, distracting her by pointing out a beautiful flower or a butterfly. "That I would have my own job, my own house, and a wife and children."

"Of course," she said. "Do your parents live very far?"

"In the next town over," he said. "Just far enough for them to not drop by randomly."

She chuckled at that. "Do you fear that?"

"Only if I'm still asleep," he replied. "My childhood nightmare would be them waking me up early in the morning."

"I used to like to sleep in as well," Emma said. "My mother always said I could sleep the day away, while she woke up at dawn."

"Mm, I know that tale," Lucas said with a smile. "What did you dream of?"

"What do you mean?" Emma asked.

"I mean, what did you dream of doing as an adult?" he asked.

"Oh," she blushed. "Not much. I just … wanted to be happy. To be a good wife and have many children. If I had to work to support my family, like my mother did, then I would. I see no shame in working hard."

"No," Lucas said. "But that is very brave of you. Many women would never consider that they were capable of working."

"Many women never had to work," Emma said quietly. "My father died when I was a baby … and …"

"I see," Lucas said. "Then your mother raised you to be strong."

"She did," Emma said with a soft smile. "She did."

They didn't make it all the way into town, because Emma grew tired. But Lucas invited her to walk again and again, and with each day, she grew stronger. She enjoyed their walks and their conversations. He always seemed to have a moment to speak to her, even when he was drowning in work.

And when she finally recovered, he once again offered her a job. Without hesitation, Emma accepted.

***

"I had to admit," Shauna said, during her first day of official work, "I wasn't sure you even knew how to make a bed."

"Of course I do," Emma said, feeling like a princess in her brand-new maid's uniform. She had never had a new dress before, and it was surprisingly comfortable. "My mother taught me well."

"I see that she did," Shauna said, watching her. "Now, I will leave you to do the rest. When you are done at noon, come down to lunch and we will plan the rest of the day."

"What else will need to be done?" Emma asked, looking around.

"It's Sunday," Shauna said. "It's our half day off."

"Oh." Her face brightened. "So … I could read in the garden?"

"Have you not read every book in the library?" Shauna asked her with a gentle smile.

"Not yet," Emma said, absolutely delighted. She couldn't remember a moment in months when she had been truly happy. However, this moment, now, reminded her of lying on the floor in the sunshine of her childhood home. She was happy, at long last.

She learned, however, that happiness didn't last. It was only three weeks later that everything shattered. She was making the beds, as she did every morning, when she heard Lucas calling through the house.

"Everyone," he said. "Everyone, I need you to come downstairs."

His voice sounded distressed, and she was worried that there was something wrong with him. Dropping what she was doing, she ran down the stairs. All the servants were rarely together, and she forgot just how many people Lucas employed. Standing in the hallway with everyone, it seemed almost crowded. Most of the time, they moved about the house like ghosts. Now, they were standing nervously, shoulder to shoulder.

"Thank you for coming so quickly," he said. "There is a matter I wanted to discuss with all of you that is quite grave."

Emma braced herself for the worst news. She imagined that he was sick, or that he was bankrupt and they would all have to leave. However, the worst thing that she could imagine didn't prepare her for what he said next.

"I regret to inform you," he said, "that several pieces of my mother's jewellery that she gave me, to give my future bride, have gone missing. At first, I thought it was just misplaced, but each day, another piece was missing. Someone has been stealing from me."

Everyone hung their head in shock. Emma felt her blood run cold.

"Now," Lucas said. "If you are stealing because you have a great need for money, or perhaps there is something happening with your family, or it's your health that you need to pay for, please do not feel that you must do this. I will support whatever you need. But this is not the way to ask for help."

Still, no one said anything. He looked each one of them in the face.

"I invite whoever did it to come forward today. There will be no punishment, no judgement, if you provide a valid reason. Please. You have until tonight."

Still, no one said anything. Emma trembled, unable to look up at him. There were people from all walks of life in the house, but she was the only one who had a background of thievery. She knew that if no one came forward, she would be blamed.

"I'll leave that with your conscience," he said quietly to the group. "And remember that I am a kind master. I understand hardship. Please do not be afraid to come forward. I shall be in my study."

And with that, he left the room.

It was a long moment before anyone spoke again.

"Well," Shauna said, turning to everyone. "I hope whoever did it comes forward. What a horrible thing to do."

Emma felt all eyes on her, and she felt her soul wither. They thought it was her. They thought she had slipped back into her old ways.

She hadn't, of course, and she never would again. But if someone didn't confess by tonight, she knew there was no hope.

She should have known that happiness was not for her.

The hours ticked by and no one confessed. She waited until everyone went to bed before she slipped into her room to pack her things, crying silently. She couldn't face Lucas in the morning knowing that he wouldn't believe the one thief he employed was innocent. She could see the disappointment in his eyes, and the pain it had caused him to even ask his staff who was guilty.

She couldn't stay. This wasn't the life that God had meant for her. Clearly, she wasn't meant to be safe and warm. She was meant to stay lowborn, and fight for survival.

***

It was just before dawn when Emma slipped out the door, not knowing where she was going to go. She was exhausted, and she felt like she had already cried a river. She knew that by leaving, she was practically admitting her guilt. She knew in their minds, she was guilty, and she had no fight left in her to convince them of her innocence.

The worst part of leaving was not the regret of leaving her comfortable life. The worst part of leaving was the fact that she was leaving a piece of her heart behind. Emma had never said anything to anyone, but her heart had warmed towards her master. He was kind and handsome and he always had a moment for her. She knew that her feelings would never be returned, but she had started to fall in love with him. She felt comfortable and safe in his presence, and she often waited eagerly for him to come home from work, just to know he was in the same house as her. Being heartbroken on two levels was more than she thought she could survive. She was certain that her last days were upon her, even as she tried to figure out her next move.

She wandered the streets for quite a while until she found herself on the outskirts of town. There were crowds out here, walking towards large buildings, and she realized she was in the factory district. The men and women whirling around her were going to work, just as her mother had before her.

The factory that her mother had worked at was long since closed, but several others had popped up in its place. Emma walked as if underwater into the nearest one that she saw other women heading into. She knew she would be a likely candidate for work, given that work in the town house had made her plump and strong and healthy. She wouldn't swoon on the work line, as so many desperate women did.

"Please," she said, to a passing worker. "Is the foreman around?"

"Right there," the woman, several years older than her, with sunken eyes, looked her up and down. "Are you looking for work?"

"Yes," Emma said. "Is this place hiring?"

"Always," the woman said, shaking her head. "Good luck to you,"

Emma didn't heed the warning, heading towards the man that had been pointed out.

"Excuse me, sir," she said. "I am looking for work."

"You ever worked in a factory before?" he said gruffly.

"No," Emma said. "But my mother did. I know what to do."

"Really?" He raised an eyebrow. "You look strong."

"I am," Emma lied. "And I work hard."

"I'll give you a try," he said. "You got a baby at home? There will be no leaving early."

"No," Emma said, her heart breaking all over again. "I have no one at home. I have no one who needs me."

"That's what I like to hear." The man grinned, showing several broken teeth. "Come with me."

Emma didn't look at anyone as she followed him to the office, where he went over the job and the measly pay packet she would receive at the end of the week.

"Suits you?" he asked at the end of it, and then laughed. "Not that it matters. There's so little work in this town."

"Suits me," Emma said. "When can I start?"

"Today," he said, pointing back out the door. "The other girls will show you your place on a line."

"Thank you," Emma said emotionlessly. This would be her life now. Happiness was not for people like her.

Chapter 7

She didn't even know what day it was. She didn't even care. Every day was the same—every moment, every sunrise, every sunset. Misery and cold was just her way of life.

Emma got up at the same time every day and went to bed at the same time every day. She slept a dreamless sleep and she didn't care about anything except working, eating enough to survive, and sleeping. The world had become grey to her in the three years she had worked at the factory.

Frankly, she was surprised that she had lasted three years at all. She had been prepared for something to go wrong, as it had every time she got comfortable in a job.

However, so far, she seemed to be able to keep her head down and out of trouble. No one was really her friend, but no one spoke negatively of her either. She was just there; just another worker in a sea of faces.

She dragged herself to work as she did every day. However, this time, someone approached her. Her foreman, Don, tapped her shoulder.

"Emma," he said. "There's someone looking for you."

"What?" she asked, surprised. "Who?"

"I don't know," he said. "Some man. Said he's been trying to track you down for some time."

Emma felt her blood run cold at that statement. Every day she thought of Lucas and the wonderful time she had at his house. However, she also looked over her shoulder, frequently wondering if he was going to send someone after her for the thievery that he suspected her of. The thievery that, she assumed, he thought she was guilty of.

"Did he say why?" she said.

"No," Don said. "Why, is there some reason why someone would be looking for you?"

"No," Emma said, even though she knew there was some reason. Of course, she didn't know for sure that it was someone from Lucas' house. However, she couldn't think of any other reason why someone would be looking for her. Nobody cared about her, unless it was in a negative way, it seemed.

"You know I don't like people causing trouble around here," he said.

"I know," Emma said. "I will make sure that there's no trouble here."

***

Emma felt like she couldn't concentrate all day. She couldn't exactly ask for more details because she was sure that would make her look guilty. However, she kept looking over her shoulder, and at the end of the day, she couldn't take it anymore.

"Do you know … what that man looked like?" she asked Don.

"I don't know," he said with a shrug. "A man, younger, dark hair."

"Did he have green eyes?" Emma asked, and Don leered at her.

"I don't know," Don answered. "Why would I notice that?"

"I apologize," Emma said. "I'm sorry."

"I thought you said that there wasn't going to be any trouble?" Don said.

"There won't be," Emma said, picking up her bag and scurrying away. Her heart was beating a million miles a minute, and she felt like she might swoon out of panic.

"Emma?"

When she heard his voice outside the factory, she did swoon. Her knees buckled and she stumbled. Luckily, Lucas reached out to catch her.

"I'm sorry, I'm sorry," she babbled. "It wasn't me, but I thought you would think it was me. I swear on my mother's grave that it wasn't me. I swear that …"

"Emma, calm down," he said. "It's all right. Everything is all right."

She couldn't believe that he was standing in front of her again. He looked just as handsome as she remembered. In fact, if it was possible, he looked even more handsome than before.

"I'm sorry," she said again, tears streaming down her face.

"I know that it wasn't you," he said. "It was Shauna. And I've been looking for you ever since."

Her jaw dropped.

"Shauna?" she said. "The housemaid?"

"Yes," he replied. "It turned out that she was building a nest egg and was about to quit."

"But … why?" Emma asked. "You treated everyone so well. You …"

He shook his head.

"It doesn't matter. It was so many years ago. I have forgiven her, and I hear she has married and gone to France."

"Oh my goodness," Emma said, still in shock.

"And you?" he asked, gazing into her eyes. "You've been here all this time?"

"I've … worked," she said.

"Are you happy?" he asked. "I can't believe that I have found you."

"It's a life," she said, avoiding his gaze. She still felt ashamed in his presence, because of the way she'd left. "And I am alive."

"Simply drawing breath is not living," he said softly. "When you left abruptly, I knew exactly what you were thinking. Shauna did too, and that was why she confessed. We searched for you for years, but we couldn't find you."

"I tried to keep my head down," she said. "So I wouldn't be found."

"Well, I'd say you did a very good job," he said. "And I don't mean to interrupt any life that you have. But … if you are interested in returning to me … and my house … I mean, the job that was yours … I would be delighted to have you."

"What?" she stammered. "Do you mean it?"

"Of course I mean it," he said. "I never found anyone as talented or as pleasant as you."

She gaped like a fish.

"But I'm … I'm not special, sir."

"On the contrary," he said. "I think that you are quite special indeed, and I would be honoured if you would consider returning. Perhaps I should give you some time to think about?"

"No," Emma blurted out, and Lucas looked shocked. "I mean, yes. I don't need time to think about it. I would love to come back and work for you. I have dreamed about such a moment, when I dared to dream. I would be honoured."

"Wonderful," he said. "What do you need?"

"I need … to give my notice," she said. "I have worked here for three years, and it feels rude to just quit."

"You have a good heart," he said. "Would you like me to escort you inside?"

"Yes," Emma said, giggling as he held out his arm. "That would be lovely."

She went inside, and she knew everyone was staring. However, she didn't care as she went to talk to Don, who simply raised an eyebrow.

"So you want … to give your notice?" he said.

"I can give you whatever notice you like," Emma said. "Is two weeks all right? I want to be respectable and …"

Don smiled for the first time in years. Emma realized that she had seen him leer and seen him look amused, but he had never, in all these years, full-on smiled.

"Go on, Emma," he said. "At least someone has a chance in this wretched place."

"Right … now?" she said. "But that's not two weeks."

"Well, you hardly need a reference, do you?" he said, glancing at Lucas. "I'll be sorry to lose a good worker."

"Emma is a good worker," Lucas agreed. "I would be happy to pay you for the honour of letting her break her contract?"

"Just go," Don said. "Get out of here, be happy, and all of that."

"Thank you," Emma said. "Thank you."

She hadn't really made any friends in her time working here, but her good mood caused her to say goodbye to a few of the women who had worked beside her.

"Where do you live?" Lucas asked as they walked out.

"A little flat that I rent by the week," she said. "I actually had to pay rent tomorrow so there will be no harm in telling that I am just going to leave. It's very cheap and there are several people who are desperate to fill it. It's just this way."

She was practically skipping down the street, arm in arm with him. She couldn't believe this was really happening.

Lucas helped her pack up her things, all while updating her on the goings on in his household. He told her about the new people that had come to work for him, and some of the older ones that had moved on. He talked about his job, and he talked about his colleagues. However, the more he talked, the more she noticed he didn't mention a family.

"How is your … family?" she asked at last. She was certain that he was married by now, to a wife who loved him and knew how lucky she was.

"My parents are well," he said.

She waited impatiently, looking at him. "That's all? There's no … you're not married?"

"Not yet," he said, and gazed at her in a way that sent shivers down her spine.

She didn't have much to pack up, and he helped her put it in two sacks that she had stored in a corner. He offered to carry both of them, but she insisted on taking one as they walked.

"Factory work has made me strong," she said, and he smiled.

"I see that," he said. "I am glad that you thrived."

"I wouldn't call it thriving," she said. "I learned to be strong because there was no one else to be strong for me."

"I am sorry that you went through that," he said. "And I am sorry that I didn't find you with more haste. You didn't deserve to feel that way, Emma. I should have hired a detective. I should have …"

"It's all right," she assured him. "We are together now, and that is all that matters."

"Yes," he agreed at last, gazing into her eyes. "That is what matters."

When she saw the town house come into view again, she breathed a sigh of relief. She had avoided walking past it all these years because she was worried about being caught. However, she had dreamed about standing in front of it most days, hoping for a miracle that she was sure would never be granted.

"Welcome home," he said to her.

"Home," she echoed in relief. She truly felt like she was home, at long last.

Chapter 8

As soon as they got settled into the town house, Emma was relieved to feel that everything felt the same. She got to stay in her old room, and most of the faces were familiar. However, there was one thing that was a little different. Lucas was just a little bit kinder, and a little bit friendly. He offered many walks into town, and seemed to want to spend time with her when she wasn't working. Emma was delighted, of course, because she had missed him very much. However, at the same time, she was a bit worried that perhaps his intentions were not as they seemed. She still was not very good at trusting people, and as much as she thought she loved Lucas, she knew they could never properly be together.

"I was wondering," Lucas said to her one day, "whether you would perhaps like to pack a picnic lunch?"

"A picnic lunch?" she said. It was early in the morning and she had barely gotten started on her chores. "I can do that. Is there anything in particular that your guests like to eat?"

"I don't know," he said with a small smile. "What is it that you like to eat?"

"That I like to … Oh." She suddenly realized what he was asking. "Oh. You want me to go on a picnic with you?"

"Yes," he said. "That was my intention."

"Oh my," she blushed. "Is there any particular reason? Am I in trouble? Are you going to fire me?"

"No!" he cried, shocked. "I just had the day off and it's beautiful outside. I thought that you would enjoy taking a stroll and enjoying the sunshine."

"I think that would be lovely," she said. "Thank you so much."

"Pack whatever you like," he said. "I'm sure I will enjoy anything you like to eat."

There were titters among the servants as she packed lunch. She knew that she got preferential treatment from Lucas, and she was worried that the opportunity to be alone with him might not be proper. However, she was too excited about the fact that she was going to have an interrupted hour to talk to him. Once the lunch was packed in the picnic basket, she met him outside in the sunshine.

"Oh," she said, looking up at the sky. "It's a lovely day."

"It is indeed," he said, offering his arm. She loved taking his arm; it was so strong and firm, and she felt completely safe when she was with him. "When I saw the weather today, I knew that I had to take time off today."

"You took the day off just for this?" she said. "I feel very blessed."

"Well, I'll admit that I was hoping you would agree," he said. "However, I couldn't possibly just ignore the sunshine. I believe that life is short and we should take advantage of each opportunity we get."

"I wish I believed the same," Emma said. "But opportunity does not come to all of us. I don't feel, aside from you, I've ever had an opportunity. I've always just had to make the best of each situation. And the best … was not very good."

"Oh, Emma," he turned to her. "I know that you've had a hard life. But I've always admired your resistance through it. You've chosen to survive, when many others would not."

"I feel like my mother would be disappointed in me if I didn't," Emma said. "She always fought for what we had, and taught me to do the same. Even when it was easier to give up …"

He laid a gentle kiss on her cheek, which surprised her. She turned to him, and she found herself with his lips on hers. It was quick and chaste, but it made her blush all the same.

"Oh my," she said.

"I'm sorry," he said. "If that was … unwanted. I've just been wanting to do that since I first saw you. And now that I've found you again, I couldn't resist."

"I …" she touched her lips.

"I won't do it again," he assured her. "We've come out to enjoy this picnic and that is what we are going to do."

She didn't know what to say. It wasn't that she didn't want his chaste kisses, but she was alone in the middle of a field with him, and she was well aware of what men could do.

The picnic was quite enjoyable, and the two of them seemed to fall into a pattern. On his days off, they would come up with reasons to sneak off, and then he would steal a chaste kiss again, and immediately apologize. She didn't tell him to stop, but she didn't tell him to continue either.

She was completely in love with him, but she knew that such a union was not possible. So instead, she fell into the rhythm alongside him, allowing herself to live in a fantasy that she knew could never play out.

There was one day, however, that felt different. Lucas had given everyone in the house the day off, and she wasn't aware of that fact until she came down the stairs in the morning. The house was silent, and he was sitting in the dining room without any food.

"My goodness, have they all absconded?" she asked with a smile.

"No," he said. "I asked them to head down to the fair in town; to take some time off. But now, the two of us are alone."

"Oh," she said, standing just a few feet apart from him. "Perhaps I should … prepare your breakfast then."

"You can," he said. "But I'm not hungry right now. I thought we could enjoy some time together instead."

"You're not hungry?" she said, immediately concerned. "Are you ill?"

"No, I'm not ill," he said. "Come and sit with me, Emma."

She froze, looking at the chair beside him.

"I would prefer to stand," she said.

"Emma," he said, looking disappointed. "Have I done something to upset you? I thought we were progressing quite well."

"Progressing?" she said.

"In our … relationship?"

She looked down at her hands.

"I just … I just … am aware of what men can do. And now we are alone in the house … and… I'm sorry. I don't want to think badly of you, but …"

"Oh my," he said. "I really never intended to give you such an impression of me."

"It's not you," she blurted out. "Really, it's just …"

"I know," he said. "You've had such a terrible life, and I want to change that for you."

"You want to … change it?" she asked, confused. "We can't change the past."

"I know," he said, going to take her hands. "I know. And I want to assure you that my intentions are honourable. I'd like to make an honest woman out of you, if you'll let me."

She knew what those words meant, individually, but it seemed odd to hear them coming from his mouth.

"I …" she said, and he reached into his pocket, and then sank to one knee.

"Emma Walker," he said. "Will you do me the honour of being my wife?"

"I …" her mind felt completely muddled and she stared at him in shock. "You want me to marry you?"

"Yes," he said. "I would be the happiest man in the world if you said yes."

"Yes," she blurted out, her smile stretching over her whole face. "Yes, yes, yes!"

He opened the box and she saw the most beautiful ring she had ever seen in her whole life. It was simple, a gold band with a diamond in it, and yet it was perfect for her. He slipped it on her finger and it fit perfectly. He then stood up and kissed her gently.

"Why me?" she asked him, still shaking. "Why … I mean, I'm not …"

"You are the most perfect woman I have ever encountered," he said. "You are the strongest, purest soul, and I would be honoured to have you by my side. And you are beautiful. Any man would be lucky to have you."

"What will people say though?" she asked.

"I don't care what people say," he said. "You are the woman I want to spend the rest of my life with."

He wrapped his arms around her and she allowed him to give her a long hung. She felt completely safe and at home in his arms, and she never wanted to break the embrace. Finally, he pulled back with a smile on his face.

"You should probably … take that off," he said, indicating her uniform. She turned bright red.

"What?"

"Oh, no, no no." He also turned bright red when he realized what he was saying. "That's not what I meant, please forgive me. What I meant was that now that you are going to marry me, you are going to be the lady of the house. You are no longer my servant."

"Oh," she said, breathing a sigh of relief. "Should I … I mean, I should probably keep working until we are married? Or at least until we find a replacement to hire? To tell you the truth, I've worked since I was twelve years old. I wouldn't know what to do."

"You can do that if you prefer," he said. "But I'm sure I'll manage."

"Well …" she said. "Perhaps just until you hire your replacement. To ease the transition in the house."

"I will leave you to pick your replacement, if you like," he said. "Find someone that you are happy with."

"That is so kind of you," she said.

"I would like to tell my parents in person," he said. "Whenever you are comfortable doing so."

"Oh," she said. "Do you think … I mean, of course, but do you think they will approve?"

"They will see how much I love you," he said. "And everything will be fine."

Under his beautiful smile, she felt completely comfortable.

"We can go whenever you like," she said. "For now … I think I will make us breakfast. I'm starving."

He chuckled at that. "Now that you have accepted, I think I would enjoy some breakfast. I was so nervous."

"You were nervous?" she asked. "Why?"

"Because … you might decline," he said. "And I don't think I could live without you."

"That is the kindest thing that anyone has ever said to me," she said. "I have never felt … wanted."

"You are very wanted," he assured her. "But I would also enjoy breakfast made by my future wife. I will cherish it."

She couldn't stop staring down at her finger, where the ring was.

"I love you," Lucas blurted out, and she looked up, meeting his eyes.

"I love you too," she said. She headed into the kitchen, humming under her breath. Her ring sparkled in the sunshine, and she couldn't believe that this was reality. She kept thinking that it was a dream that she was going to wake up from.

***

When the others finally came home, she told them the news right away. To her surprise, everyone was very supportive. They were happy, and congratulated her. She rejoined Lucas later, discussing plans for their wedding. He sent a note to his parents, indicating that he would like to visit in the next few days, and that he had big news. The letter came back after lunch inviting him to come next week, for a meal, and that they couldn't wait to hear what the news was.

"Are you sure they'll accept me?" Emma asked.

"Of course they will," Lucas said. "They've only ever wanted me to be happy, and I am the happiest man in the world with you by my side."

Chapter 9

Emma was nervous as they pulled up to his parents' house. However, she was assured by Lucas several times, and she tried to put on a smile as they knocked on the door.

She had seen Lucas' parents only once before, when they had visited briefly. She had been mostly in the kitchen, and she hadn't said a word to them. She was sure they wouldn't even remember her. This time, however, she was standing on their doorstep and holding their son's hand.

When the door opened, Emma put on her brightest smile. His father looked excited, until he saw her.

"Lucas?" he said. "What is this?"

She noted that he didn't even greet his son.

"This is Emma," Lucas said. "And she is my fiancée."

"Lucas, this is your housemaid." His father's eyes practically bugged out of his head. "Is this some kind of cruel joke?"

"No," Lucas said, staring right at his father. "This is my fiancée and the woman I love. May we come in?"

His father's eyes flickered in between Emma and Lucas. Then the man stood tall.

"Lucas," he said. "You have always been a disobedient son. But if you say this is not some sort of joke, I will not allow you to cross this doorstep."

"What?" Lucas said, reacting in shock. "Emma is …"

"You have already brought this family's name down with all of the deplorables that you hang around with. But now you want to tell me that you are going to take one of them as your bride? This cannot be."

Emma's lip trembled. "I'm sorry, sir," she said. "I should have never …"

"No," her future father-in-law turned to her. "This is not your fault. You just wanted my son's money. He should have better judgement."

"I have perfect judgement," Lucas said. "And I assure you, Emma is the most perfect …"

Emma felt her heart sink. She felt her stomach pitch down to her feet. She felt like she couldn't breathe.

She would give anything to have had this moment go well. She knew what was going to happen and her heart broke as she watched the next few moments unfold.

He didn't even get to finish his sentence. The door closed in his face, with a final shout from his father.

"I will disown you," he said, and the door practically broke from the force that he slammed it with.

Emma immediately had tears streaming down her face. Lucas' face was bright red with anger.

"I can't believe him," he said. "I can't believe that he …"

"Lucas, he's right," Emma said. "You are marrying below your station and I will …"

"On the contrary," he said, turning to her. "I am marrying above my station. Your soul is beautiful and you are a better, stronger person than I am. I will never find anyone else like you."

She couldn't stop crying, and he wrapped his arms around her.

"It's all right," he assured her. "Really, it's all right. We'll figure it out."

"Lucas, he said he was going to disown you!" Emma cried. "How can you …"

"He won't," Lucas said. "And if he does, that is his problem, not mine. You know that I am independently wealthy, Emma. I don't need my parents."

"Do you know what I would give to have parents?" she blurted out. "I would give anything in the world to have my parents here with me. And you are just …"

"I will not choose between my parents and the woman I love," he said, looking right into her eyes. "I won't. They are making their choice. I admit, they are in a bit of a shock. But they will come around. They are reasonable people."

"I can't—" her heart broke, and she sobbed into his shoulder.

"Why don't we go for a walk?" he said. "You've never seen the market in this town, and perhaps we could take a walk around before we headed home."

"I …" she couldn't even think straight; she was crying so hard. She couldn't even breathe, and he embraced her again.

"It's all right," he said. "Take all the time you need. We'll do whatever you like."

Eventually, Emma agreed to walk around with him. Neither of them discussed what had just happened, but she had a feeling that it wasn't just going to away.

Lucas pretended that it didn't matter to him. However, he clearly had a dark cloud around him all afternoon. He took her to lunch and eventually, he took her home, and pretended that everything had gone well.

Emma, however, cried herself to sleep that night, hoping that no one could hear her. She couldn't stand the fact that she was driving a wedge between him and his family.

***

Lucas' father sent a letter the next day, and confirmed exactly what he'd said at the door.

"How dare he," Lucas said. "How dare he say such things?"

"He just wants what is best for his family," Emma said, absolutely dejected as she sat in the chair opposite him. She felt like she couldn't cry anymore. Her eyes were red and her head pounded in exhaustion.

"He doesn't understand what is best for my family and what I am trying to build," Lucas responded, and then looked up at her. "You're not eating anything."

She sighed. "I just …"

"Emma, please don't let this bother you," he begged her, reaching across the table to take her hands. "Really, it's all right. We will get married no matter what happens. If they don't come around, then I will proudly stand at the end of the aisle and marry you without him standing there."

"You can't do that," Emma said. "Your parents need to be there."

"No," he said. "They really don't. If I never talk to them again, but I have you by my side, then I will be more than happy."

Emma couldn't say anything to that because her heart was breaking. His words weighed heavily on her, and she lay awake that night, staring at the wall.

She had no family, and she missed them every single day. She thought family was one of the most precious things that anyone had. She couldn't drive a wedge between them.

Emma felt like her life had been a series of running away. First there had been Mrs. Joffrey, and then the pickpockets. She had already left this house once, when Shauna had stolen jewellery, and now she knew she had to do it again. She knew that it was too good to be true. She couldn't stay here and cause Lucas to choose between her and his parents.

She made a plan, and packed her bags in the middle of the night. As soon as Lucas went to work, she was going to leave. What she didn't count on was him knocking on her door before he left for work.

"Emma?" he said. "I just wanted to give you these."

In his hand there was a box full of jewellery.

"My mother gave me these to give to my future wife," he said. "And you would honour me by wearing them, to show you are now part of my family."

She stared at him in shock.

"I can't," she said. "I can't wear them. Not with everything that is going on."

"My darling," he said. "She didn't say that she had to approve of my future bride. They belong to you; this was the intent."

"I can't." She shook her head, the tears falling again. Her heart was beating hard, and she was worried that he would notice that she had a bag packed in the corner of the room.

He looked upon her with sadness, and then placed the box at the end of the bed.

"I would like you to have them," he said. "But I understand your choice. Try to smile today, my love," he said. He kissed her on the forehead and then headed out to work.

***

Emma stared at the box for such a long time. The jewels were beautiful, and in another moment, she would have loved to wear them. But today, she knew she had to leave them aside.

As soon as she heard him leave, she crawled out of bed and went to get dressed. She put on the dress that she'd had on when she arrived, and made sure to slip her engagement ring off of her finger. It broke her heart to leave it, but she thought that he should have it back if they weren't getting married.

If she left now, he would have a chance at a new life. He would hopefully be able to forget her, and mend the relationship with his family.

She didn't know where she was going to go, but she knew she was leaving.

The actual act of leaving was trickier than she realized. Her heart was pounding, and there were several servants moving around. She didn't want to talk to anyone, and she especially didn't want anyone to see her tear streaked face.

She waited until they were setting the dining room for lunch, and then picked up her bag and slipped out the door.

"Miss Emma?" someone called, but she shut the door behind her and started down the street.

She couldn't bring herself to turn around. If she turned around, she would lose her courage.

Emma had some money with her, from when she had been Lucas' housemaid, and she planned to find a room in an inn. After that, she planned to go back to the factories and see if Don would rehire her. She was worried that she would meet the same fate as her mother, but part of Emma didn't care anymore. If she couldn't be with Lucas, she wasn't sure life was worth living.

"How long will you stay?" the innkeeper asked. "And I want you to know that this is a respectable establishment. There will be no disrespectful business taking place in your room."

"I don't know how long I will stay," Emma said, barely able to speak. "But I have nowhere else to go. I plan to get a job in the factories."

"A woman like you?" She looked her up and down. "Have you ever worked in a factory?"

"I have," she said. "I know I don't look like it anymore but … I have."

"And you'll really be all alone in your room?"

"Yes," Emma said. "I don't have anyone else."

The innkeeper looked her up and down again and then held out her hand for a few coins.

"You can stay for a week for that," the innkeeper said. "New rent is due within one day of the week expiring or I will have you hauled out on the street. There is no funny business here."

"I understand," Emma said.

"You should cheer up, girly," the innkeeper said. "At least you can afford to pay for a room. Do you know how many people can't?"

"It's just … not the life I'm used to," Emma said. "At least, not anymore."

"Oh I see," said the innkeeper. "You've fallen from grace, have you?"

"You might say that," Emma replied. "I've …" She couldn't tell her story, without crying.

"You don't owe me an explanation, dearie," the woman said. "You are not the first one to come in here down on her luck with a story. Just head up to your room, keep your head down, and you'll be all right."

"Thank you," Emma said. "Thank you very much."

The room was small, and it was cold. But it was all Emma needed in order to sleep and find a new job. This was her life now. And somehow, she felt like it had always been meant to be her life. She wasn't destined for happiness. She wasn't even sure she was destined to survive.

Chapter 10

"Sir, it's Emma," Lucas heard someone say as he sat bolt upright in bed.

"What?" he asked, wiping the sleep from his eyes.

"It's Emma," someone said again, and he woke up more, to find his footman standing there.

"What do you mean, it's Emma?" he asked. "Is something wrong? Is she sick? Dear God, call a doctor if she's sick! I'll go there right now. I'll …"

"She's not sick, sir," the footman said. "She's gone."

"She's GONE?" Lucas immediately thought the worst. "What do you mean she's gone? She's dead?"

He feared the absolute worse. He worried that Emma had fallen or gotten sick in the middle of the night and he would never see her again. He was terrified that he would never get to tell her all the things he was thinking, or share all the beautiful moments that he'd dreamed about with her.

"I don't know if she's dead, sir," the footman said. "But she's not in the house any longer."

Lucas took a minute to process this, and then realized what had happened.

"Oh no," he said. "She's done it again. I want every servant woken up, and we are going to search the city."

"The city is very big, sir," the footman said.

"It is," Lucas said. "But Emma won't be far. She's on foot and she's likely gone to one of the inns in town."

"Right," the footman said, calculating how many inns there were. He came to a number in the double digits, and groaned inwardly. "You stay here, sir, and we'll …"

"Stay here?" Lucas looked positively appalled. "I don't think so."

"Oh," the footman said.

"I'm going to find her," Lucas said. "And you are all going to help."

***

Lucas hadn't quite realized how many inns were in town, despite his staff's warning. However, that didn't stop him from running up and down the street and bursting into each inn, trying to find her. The innkeepers seemed more and more annoyed with each outburst, although he thought that was possibly due to the fact that his search was getting more frantic as the night went on.

"Maybe I was wrong," he said to the footman, somewhere around 3:00 in the morning. "Maybe I was wrong and Emma is just not here. Maybe she's gone. Maybe …"

"There are still a few more places," the footman replied, without much hope. "Let me show you."

Lucas felt like he was going to drop somewhere near dawn. However, when he walked into what was the last inn, he stopped cold.

There, standing in the morning rays of sunshine, clearly headed out for the day, was Emma. She looked as exhausted as he felt, but she was standing there, alive and well.

"Emma?" he asked, and she turned to him in shock.

"Lucas?" she said. "What are you doing here?"

"What am I doing here?" he echoed, dumbfounded. "I'm looking for you. My God, Emma, I thought you were dead or worse."

"Might be better if I was," she replied, tears coming to her voice.

"What are you talking about?" he asked, taking a step towards her. "Of course it wouldn't be better if you were dead. It would be a disaster. I would be brokenhearted."

"More brokenhearted than if you never spoke to your parents again?" she asked, and his face softened.

"Emma, darling," he said. "Is that what this is about?"

The tears that welled up in her eyes told him that it was. He took another gentle step closer, and she didn't move away.

"You can't run like this every time," he said. "Because I will always come and find you. I love you, Emma, and I will never just leave you to survive in this world alone."

"I can't do it, Lucas," she said as the tears slipped onto the floor. "I can't be the reason that you don't have a family. I spent most of my life wishing for a family, wishing I had what you do. I won't be the cause of that destruction."

"You're right," he said, to the surprise of everyone who was now eavesdropping. "But not in the way you think. If you leave me, you will be the reason I won't have a family. Because, Emma Walker, you are my family. You are my soul mate, and my one true desire. If I don't have you, I am truly alone."

She was stunned by his words. No one had ever said such things to her before. No one had ever needed her in such a way before.

"Really?" she managed at last.

"Yes," he said. "Really."

Their eyes met and Emma took a cautious step towards Lucas.

"So, my dear," he asked. "Will you come home?"

"Home?" She seemed to be lost for words.

"To my home," he clarified. "Which is your home too. In fact, it's not a home without you in it. So what do you say?"

"I …" she said.

"Please." He took her hands, staring straight into her eyes. She could not resist his gaze; not when he looked at her like that. "Please."

"Yes," she said at last. "Yes, I will."

He squeezed her hands and beamed with joy.

"Well then, my dear," he said. "You've made me the happiest man in the world."

The entire eavesdropping population of the inn burst into applause, despite the early hour. Emma blushed, and leaned into Lucas.

"I still have things upstairs," she said. "Should I …"

"I'll get them," he said. "And when I come back, we shall never be apart again."

That sounded like the best thing Emma had heard in her whole life. She watched as Lucas headed up the stairs, love in her eyes. There weren't very many people in the world who could change her mind on a dime, but clearly, Lucas had a power over her that she never wanted to forsake.

He came down with her satchel, and then took her hand and led her outside.

"Where were you going?" he asked as they walked.

"I was going to try and get a job," Emma said. "But really, I was wondering how I was going to be able to breathe without you by my side."

"You won't ever have to wonder that again," Lucas promised, escorting her toward home. Emma looked at the path in front of them. When she had last walked it, it had seemed dingy, dusty, and impossibly long. But now, with Lucas on her arm and her mind set on home, she thought she could walk every day by his side. "You will still marry me, won't you?"

"Yes," she said, gazing into his eyes. "I will."

Chapter 11

Emma had been afraid to dream of this day like other little girls had. She had always hoped that she'd be a bride one day, but she was sure that no one would want to marry her. She had seen other weddings before, and admired the beautiful brides that came out of the church.

Of course, life was different for her compared to the other brides that had gotten married in the church. The priest had been awkward when she explained that she had no father to walk her down the aisle, and that her mother would not be there to dress her. She had assured him that she'd be all right on her own, but that didn't mean she could ignore the hole that was in her heart in the moments before she was due to walk down the aisle. She wanted more than anything for her father to take her arm, or for her mother to help put her veil over her face. However, she knew that both things would only happen in her dreams.

Instead, she glanced at herself one last time in the mirror, and adjusted her veil. After today, there was one consolation. She was never going to be alone again. Lucas would always be there for her. Whatever obstacles life presented, they would navigate them together.

"Hello, dear." A kindly old woman knocked on the door. "I just came to see if you were ready. Everyone is here."

"Is Lucas here?" she asked.

The old woman smiled. "Yes, he's here," she said. "Don't worry. He looks very excited, by the way. I wish you all the happiness in the world."

In the church, there were many friendly faces waiting for them. She had tried to track down as many of the orphans as she could, and tried to send invitations to those who weren't in the city any more. Not everyone had come, but she was happy to see that many of them had, and they looked happy and fit. She was glad that she wasn't the only one who had had life turn out all right. Some of them looked like they were positively thriving, which made her beam as she walked down the aisle.

However, all it took was one look at Lucas to know that she truly belonged at the end of the aisle with him. He looked stunningly handsome in his well-tailored suit. From the way he looked at her, in her conservative lace gown, she could tell that he felt as in love with her as she did with him.

"Hello, my love," he said, when she finally got to the end of the aisle. "I have been waiting for you."

"I'll never keep you waiting again," she promised him as he lifted her veil. He took her hands and squeezed gently, giving her courage. The church was very large, and she never liked standing up in front of large groups of people. However, now, gazing into Lucas' eyes, she knew that she was safe and all would be well.

"Are you ready to start?" he asked her, and she nodded. In rehearsal yesterday, they had gone over everything several times. However, she still felt nervous. She knew that she didn't have to say many lines and that he would be there to help her if anything happened. Her hands felt sweaty and she squeezed his own to take one more ounce of courage before the priest cleared his throat and began the ceremony.

"Dearly beloved, we have come together in the presence of God to witness and bless the joining together of this man and this woman in holy matrimony. The bond and covenant of marriage was established by God in creation, and our Lord Jesus Christ adorned this manner of life by His presence and first miracle at the wedding in Cana of Galilee. It signifies to us the mystery of the union between Christ and His church, and holy scripture commends it to be honoured among all people. The union of husband and wife is intended by God for their mutual joy; for the help and comfort given each other in prosperity and adversity; and, when it is God's will, for the procreation of children and their nurture in the knowledge and love of the Lord. Therefore marriage is not to be entered into unadvisedly or lightly, but reverently, deliberately, and in accordance with the purposes for which it was instituted by God."

When he had started reading in rehearsal, Emma had almost bolted down the aisle thinking of the hundreds of pairs of her eyes looking at her. Now, it seemed everything disappeared. All she could see was Lucas' face, and his kind eyes. She hadn't thought that she would ever feel this kind of love. She'd thought love stories like this were reserved for people who had money; who were lucky and destined for good things. And yet, here she was.

"Into this union Emma Walker and Lucas Clarke now come to be joined. If any of you can show just cause why they may not be lawfully wed, speak now, or else forever hold your peace."

She was sure that there were several reasons why they shouldn't marry. They were very different people, and she was sure that someone in the crowd would at least half-heartedly shout something out. But no one did. She breathed a sigh of relief and Lucas raised an eyebrow at her.

"Did you really think that anyone would say a word?" he asked.

"No," she said, and then blushed. "Perhaps."

"No one will ever say a word against you again," he promised her. "We will forever be one, and anyone who says a word against you speaks against me as well."

"I love you," she said. "I know I should wait until the end of the ceremony to say that but …"

"I love you too," he said, and the priest cleared his throat.

"May I continue?" he asked, and both of them nodded, feeling like scolded schoolchildren.

"Thank you," the priest said, and then looked back to the book in front of him.

"I charge you both, here in the presence of God and the witness of this company, that if either of you know any reason why you may not be married lawfully and in accordance with God's Word, you now confess it."

"No." She remembered that this was one of the times that they were supposed to speak, and breathed a sigh of relief. She also correctly remembered what she was supposed to say in answer to this question. "There is absolutely no reason why we shouldn't be married."

"No," Lucas repeated. His voice was strong and echoed through the church. "There is absolutely no reason why we shouldn't be married."

The priest than turned to her and she felt shivers down her spine. In rehearsal, she had been nervous when these words were said to her. Now, she felt positively terrified and yet excited at the same time.

"Emma Walker, will you have this man to be your husband; to live together with him in the covenant of marriage? Will you love him, comfort him, honour and keep him, in sickness and in health; and, forsaking all others, be faithful unto him as long as you both shall live?"

"I will," she said, looking her future husband right in the eye. "I will."

"Lucas Clarke, will you have this woman to be your wife; to live together with her in the covenant of marriage? Will you love her, comfort her, honour and keep her, in sickness and in health; and, forsaking all others, be faithful unto her as long as you both shall live?"

"I will," he said, his voice still strong. He was such a comforting presence and Emma knew she would always be safe with him.

"Will all of you witnessing these promises do all in your power to uphold these two persons in their marriage?"

"We will," the congregation chorused. Emma couldn't believe that so many of them had come. She had often felt like she hadn't had friends most of her life, but the truth was that she did. There were so many friendly faces from so many different times in her life. Looking out into the congregation was like looking out into her past. She smiled at them as they promised their support. She knew the road ahead would be difficult, but once she and Lucas were married, and with all this support at their backs, she knew that they would be fine.

"Bless, O Lord, these rings as a symbol of the vows by which this man and this woman have bound themselves to each other; through Jesus Christ our Lord," the priest said, and the young ring bearer brought out the rings. They had chosen simple gold bands. It wasn't because Lucas couldn't afford more; he certainly could if Emma had desired it. But she hadn't wanted anything fancy. She didn't feel like it suited her. And in addition, she didn't feel like she needed something extravagant to tell the world that she belonged to Lucas and he to her.

The ring bearer approached Lucas first and he took Emma's ring out of the small box. She was trembling with nerves, but one look at his smile reminded her that all was well. He was going to take care of her, and this ring was the symbol that everything was going to be all right.

"I give you this ring as a symbol of my love, and with all that I am, and all that I have, I honour you, in the name of the Father, and of the Son, and of the Holy Spirit," Lucas said, slipping the ring on Emma's finger. It fit perfectly and she felt like God had made her finger to wear such a ring. She gazed at it as it sparkled in the sunlight. She hadn't realized it, but she had been waiting her whole life to wear a ring like this.

Next, the ring bearer approached Emma, and she took Lucas' ring out of the box. All she had to do was echo his words, but her voice shook as she did. This was more than just standing up and speaking in front of many people. This was a promise that was going to change her life.

"I give you this ring as a symbol of my love, and with all that I am, and all that I have, I honour you, in the name of the Father, and of the Son, and of the Holy Spirit," she said. Lucas' ring fit him perfectly as well.

"Now that Emma Walker and Lucas Clarke have given themselves to each other by solemn vows, with the joining of hands and the giving and receiving of rings, I pronounce that they are husband and wife, in the name of the Father, and the Son, and the Holy Spirit. Those whom God has joined together, let no one put asunder," the priest said, and Emma felt shudders go down her spine. This was really happening; it wasn't just a pleasant dream. She was going to be officially married to the love of her life in a few moments and no one could ever separate them again.

The priest looked out into the congregation, his voice booming with confidence.

"Let us stand and pray together the words our Saviour taught us," he said, and everyone stood up in unison.

"Our Father, who art in heaven, hallowed be thy name. Thy kingdom come, they will be done, on earth as it is in heaven. Give us this day our daily bread, and forgive us our trespasses, as we forgive those who trespass against us. And lead us not into temptation, but deliver us from evil, for thine is the kingdom, and the power, and the glory, forever. Amen."

"Amen," everyone echoed.

"God the Father, God the Son, God the Holy Spirit, bless, preserve, and keep you; the Lord mercifully with his favour look upon you, and fill you with all spiritual benediction and grace; that you may faithfully live together in this life, and in the age to come have life everlasting. Amen. The peace of the Lord be with you always," he said, and Emma felt a peace come over her as she echoed the words that the priest had blessed them all with.

"And also with you," she said, in unison with the congregation.

"Emma Walker and Lucas Clarke, having witnessed your vows of love to one another, it is my joy to present you to all gathered here as husband and wife. Lucas Clarke, you may kiss the bride."

The words hit her like a ton of bricks. This was it; they were married.

Emma let Lucas lean in and kiss her delicately on the lips. The entire congregation applauded as the two of them joined hands and walked down the aisle.

Emma grasped Lucas' hand as they walked out of the church, beaming.

"I love you," he whispered to her.

"I love you too," she said, never wanting to let go.

Chapter 12

Emma had heard many stories about what it was going to be like, giving birth. She had heard both horror stories and wonderful tales, and she was both fearful and excited. When she found out that she was with child, she was over the moon. Many of her friends in the neighbourhood were also with child, and she saw it as an opportunity to become closer to them. But one thing that she noticed was that there was family around every other woman. There were beaming mothers and proud fathers, and their husbands' parents were also quick to offer any assistance. Emma felt lonely in the town house, with just Lucas and the servants, despite the fact that he made sure that she didn't need anything at all.

"You seem so down today, my love," Lucas said one evening, close to when she was due to give birth. "What can I do? What will help?"

She sighed, staring out the window as she put her hand on her large belly.

"It isn't anything," she assured him. "I was just thinking of what my mother would be doing if she were here."

"I imagine she would give you advice," he said. "Or perhaps offer you a hot cup of tea. Your mother seemed like a very kind person, from what you have told me."

"She was," Emma said. "Although the more the years go by, the more she fades from memory."

Her husband could see that this thought distressed her, and so he frantically tried to think of what would make it better.

"Do you have any drawings of her?" he asked. "Or any pictures?"

"No," Emma replied sadly. "She died when I was young, and you know how often I moved around."

"What if I commissioned an artist?" Lucas asked, and Emma looked at him, confused.

""An artist?" she asked.

"Yes," he replied. "To draw you and then to draw your mother, as you describe her. We could hang it here on the mantelpiece."

"Oh, Lucas," Emma's eyes shone and he could tell that she very much liked that idea.

"That is too kind. But are you sure you want me drawn like this?" She indicated her swollen frame. "Perhaps we could wait …"

"I'm sure there will be many drawings of the baby," he said with a smile. "What I want is what will make you happy in the moment. And perhaps we can get another one done after the baby comes. Would you like that?"

"Yes, please," she said, and Lucas nodded.

"Wonderful," he said. "I'll arrange it."

***

Emma never doubted a word that Lucas told her, but this seemed like such a fanciful idea that she couldn't believe when a man showed up at the door three days later, with an easel and paints on his back.

"Emma," Lucas said. "This is Mr. Oriel. He's a wonderful local artist and I knew that he would be the best person to sketch you."

Emma smiled at the man who stood at the door. Despite his supplies, he stood there in ragged clothes, with paint smears on his hands and dirt under his nails. She didn't judge him for it, for she had once been in the same position. She knew that it was likely that Lucas had seen him do some drawings on the street and had commissioned him. However, she also knew that he was probably very talented. She admired her husband so much for his good deeds.

"Wonderful," she said with a smile. "It's nice to meet you, Mr. Oriel."

"And you, Mrs. Clarke," the man said. "When Mr. Clarke told me what kind of portrait you wanted, I thought it sounded thrilling. After all, drawing all comes from the heart, doesn't it?"

"I suppose so," Emma said as he walked in. "Where shall we go? Shall I change? Is my hair all right?"

Lucas chuckled at that, putting a gentle hand on her back.

"Your hair is just perfect, my dear. You are just perfect, in fact. I was thinking that the back garden would be a good place? The light is perfect right now."

"Oooh, yes," Emma said, leading him through the house.

She had never posed for an artist before, but Mr. Oriel was very easy to work with. He told her to sit however was comfortable for her and he would take care of the rest.

Emma settled on a rock in the sun, feeling sleepy from its warmth. Under Lucas' watchful eye, Mr. Oriel began to draw. The three of them fell into silence and Emma's mind drifted. She felt the baby kick inside of her, and put a hand to her belly. She was imagining a few years in the future, playing in the garden with this child, and perhaps more. This moment was perfect, and she couldn't wait to meet their future heir.

"Tell me about your mother," Mr. Oriel said, gently shaking her out of her thoughts. She turned to him.

"What would you like to know?" she asked, and Mr. Oriel shrugged with a smile.

"Anything you like," he replied. "What did she look like? What was her personality like? What did you like best about her? What do you remember best about her?"

Emma didn't know what to say at first. Her words came out hesitantly, and she could tell that she wasn't being much help at all. However, as Mr. Oriel began to put tentative sketches to paper, Emma began to feel freedom in her words.

She wasn't sure how long she talked about her mother, but her throat was soon dry and her mouth was sore from smiling. She was about to comment on that fact when she felt pain in her belly.

At first, she thought that it was kicking. However, the pain got worse and she quickly gasped.

"Emma?" Lucas asked.

"I think …" Emma said, in between sharp pains. "I think the baby is coming."

"I'm almost done," Mr. Oriel said, almost impatiently.

"I think we're going to have to finish another day," Lucas said, rushing to his wife. "Mr. Oriel, I will pay you extra if you go and fetch the midwife for us."

"Oh!" Mr. Oriel dropped his sketch pencil at once. "Right away, sir."

"Come on, Emma." Lucas gently helped her up. "Let's get you inside."

"I wish my mother was here," Emma said, as tears of fear slid down her face.

"She is here," Lucas said gently, turning her around to look at the garden. "She's here with you in spirit. Come, look at his drawing. It isn't quite finished yet, but …"

"Oh," Emma gasped when she saw it. Somehow, through all of her babbling, Mr. Oriel had managed to sort out exactly what was important. Standing behind her in the picture was a near perfect likeness of her mother, sketched in pencil and beginning to be filled in with colour. "Oh my goodness."

"Is it like her?" Lucas asked, as Emma reached out a trembling hand to touch the painting.

"Yes," she said, putting a finger on her mother's cheek. "It's just like her. OH!"

She nearly doubled over in pain again and Lucas rushed her inside the house.

"She's with you," Lucas promised her. "She's with you just like that. Everything is all right, my dear."

***

Mr. Oriel was fast, and the midwife was soon there. Emma had never felt pain like this in her life, and she cried out, gripping at the sheets and labouring for what felt like days.

She wanted her mother more than anything, and as she tossed and turned, she began to feel her mother's touch, and see her face, just beyond the painful reality that she was living.

"Is it much longer?" she asked the midwife, gasping and panting. The small but determined woman shook her head, standing at the foot of the bed.

"Won't be much longer at all, my dear," she said. "But you do need to push now."

"But my mother isn't here yet," Emma protested, half in another reality.

"PUSH!" the midwife cried, and Emma did.

True to her word, it wasn't long at all before Emma heard a piercing cry cut through the air. It brought her back to reality; her mother's face faded from her vision as it was replaced with that of a screaming baby boy.

"A boy," Emma whispered, gazing upon him. He was perfect and tiny, with blue eyes and hair the colour of straw. He looked just like Lucas, she thought. "I have a son."

"What is his name?" the midwife asked, with a smile.

"Lucas Clarke the second," Emma said, as she gazed upon her perfect child. "After his father. Lukie, for short."

"Well, Lukie, welcome to the world," the midwife said. "Do you think he might like to meet his father now?"

"Oh yes," Emma replied, struggling to sit up in bed.

Lucas rushed in the second he was allowed to, joy and nerves wracking his features.

"I'm all right," Emma assured him as she extended her arms slightly. "You have a son."

She had never seen her husband cry before. He had always been strong and stoic in the face of the waves of emotion that they had experienced. But at the sight of his son, fat tears of happiness rolled down his face.

"May I?" he asked Emma, and she nodded. Gently, he picked the bundle of blankets up from her arms and started to rock it. "Hello, baby boy," he whispered, sinking down on the bed and staring in amazement.

They had about twenty minutes alone before there was another knock on the door. Emma thought that it was the midwife, looking for her pay, and looked up in half exhaustion. However, the figure at the door shocked her.

Lucas' father stood at the door, his expression soft and meek.

"Hello, son," he said, his eyes on the baby. "I … heard the news and … your mother wanted me to make sure everything was all right. Your mother … is it a boy?"

"Yes," Lucas said, surprised to see his father there as well. "Yes, it's a boy. My son."

The three of them sat in silence, awkwardly staring at each other. George Clarke seemed much softer in this light, his shoulders rounded and his back hunched. The sight of his grandson seemed to take away all the anger that he had previously felt.

He was the last person Emma had expected to see standing at her birthing bed, and a large part of her just wanted to ask him to leave. After all, he had been absolutely horrible to them, and caused many hurt feelings.

The life that Emma lived should have hardened her. It should have made her soul dark and made her demand that Mr. Clarke simply leave the room.

However, Emma was not the person that life had tried to make her. She was kindhearted and sweet, and her mother had taught her to extend the olive branch when she could.

"Would you like to hold him?" she asked gently.

Mr. Clarke reacted in surprise. "Really?" he said.

Emma smiled. "Of course," she said. "He's your grandson, isn't he? And family is family."

Mr. Clarke looked positively ashamed of his previous actions. He nodded, and stepped forward. Lucas carefully got up and placed the baby in his father's arms.

A moment passed between them, and Emma felt like the rift could possibly heal at last.

Mr. Clarke held the baby for a long moment and then passed him back to Lucas.

"You've done a fantastic job, son," he said, and then looked between both of them. "You both have. I should have said it earlier, and I apologize for that. I am proud of both of you, and the life you've made."

"Thank you," Emma said. "But it's because of Lucas' kind heart that I am here at all."

"Yes," his father turned to him. "Despite your upbringing, Lucas, you have turned out quite well."

Lucas chose his words carefully then.

"Well," he said. "I think we can make sure my son has an upbringing that we won't have to stand here in twenty-five years and apologize for, don't you?"

George laughed at that, despite himself.

"Yes," he said. "I think we can."

"Perhaps we can have the two of you over for dinner?" Emma asked. "In a few days' time, once we are settled?"

"I would like that very much," George replied. "Thank you both. I will leave you in peace now."

"Don't be a stranger," Lucas said as he let his father out the door. Once he was gone, Emma's husband turned to her. "Well, that was a surprise."

"It was a happy surprise," she said. "And I'm glad he came."

"You are?" Lucas said.

"Yes," she said. "I really am. I think that our son's life should include his grandparents, and as much family as he can get. Family is everything."

"Yes," Lucas said. "Family is everything. And we are a family now."

"Well," Emma said, with a coy smile. "We're the start of one anyways."

Lucas raised his eyebrows.

"You want to go through all of that again so soon?"

"Maybe not right away," Emma said, gazing down at her son. "But pretty soon. It's worth it, don't you think?"

"Oh yes," Lucas said, looking at the two of them with love. "It's all worth it."

Emma knew that there would be hard days to come. However, she knew that as long as they were together, everything would be all right.

The End

More Victorian Romance by Molly Britton

The Battered Orphan

The Orphan's Distress

Printed in Great Britain
by Amazon